In My HOOD₂

BY

ENDY

In My Hood 2. Copyright © 2009 by Endy. All rights reserved. Printed in the United States of America. No part of this book may be used or reproduced in any manner whatsoever without written permission except in the case of brief quotations embodied in critical articles or reviews. For information, address Melodrama Publishing, P.O. Box 522, Bellport, NY 11713.

Library of Congress Control Number: 2009938149
ISBN-13: 978-1934157589
ISBN-10: 1934157589
Mass Market Edition: February 2010
10 9 8 7 6 5 4 3 2 1

To read excerpts, download order forms, and learn more about our titles, please visit our website at:
www.melodramapublishing.com

Interior and Cover Design by candace@candann.com

CHAPTER 1

The night wind whipped in circles, causing paper to blow about the street. A can rolled back and forth as if in the middle of a tug-of-war with the wind. The streetlights had been broken out by the drug runners in an attempt to keep darkness over the corners of Isabella Avenue and Eighteenth Avenue in Newark, New Jersey. It was two a.m. and the night was cold. Jack Frost had definitely reared his ugly head on this night. A lone car cruised up the block of Isabella, almost crawling. The two occupants of the old, worn-out, Toyota Camry both looked in the direction of the building that stood on the corner. A figure emerged from the darkness of the building's doorway and stepped out into the moonlight. The car stopped and pulled over to the corner and the young man who had emerged from the building strolled over to the car.

The young man was dressed in a pair of Roc-a-wear jeans three sizes too big, which swallowed his narrow body. Charcoal gray Timberlands swallowed his feet as he bopped along the sidewalk, dragging his feet on the pavement. His gray, Eckō, goose-down coat hung on his body like a sleeping bag. The hood on the black hoodie that he wore underneath the coat was pulled tight around a fitted cap of his head.

"What up?" he asked the passengers of the car as he stood two feet from the vehicle.

"Let me get two and two," the male passenger said, stretching his eyes.

The young man turned toward the entrance from which he had come and held up two fingers on his right hand and then two fingers on his left. He turned back to the passenger and grabbed the two, twenty-dollar bills that the passenger held out the window. After taking the money, the young hustler walked away from the car and headed toward the building. As he approached, another young man emerged from the building wearing an almost identical ensemble in blue. They bypassed each other as if they didn't know one another. The young man in blue clunked over to the car and tossed the drug purchase into the passenger's hand, and as quickly as he appeared, he disappeared even quicker.

The car drove off and rounded the corner faster than it had approached, leaving behind a trail of polluted smoke.

"Damn, it's cold out this bitch!" the young man in the gray Timberlands, whose name was Day-Day, proclaimed.

"A-Yo, man, I'm 'bout to bounce to the crib. It's slow as hell out tonight, anyway," the young man dressed in blue, whose name was Unique, said.

"Word! I'm with you. Yo, come to my crib so I can finish whooping yo' ass in NBA basketball on PlayStation 2," Day-Day said with confidence.

"Yeah a'ight nigga, and then you woke up!"

The two stood in the deep doorway of the apartment

building. Because of the darkness of the street, no casual observer would be able to see them standing there. They huddled together in an attempt to escape the harsh winds that blew about the streets.

"What time is it?" Unique asked.

Day-Day reached into his pocket and pulled out his cell phone.

"It's two-twenty. Yo, at three, that's a wrap."

"Cool, I'm wit' that," Unique agreed.

"A-Yo, kid, did you ever fuck that girl we met outside the strip joint the other night?"

"Naw, son. When I was talking to shorty, I saw she had a sore in the corner of her mouth. That shit turned my stomach. I wasn't sticking my dick in her mouth or in her pussy," Unique said, frowning.

"Ill, that shit is nasty. Shorty was fire, too. That trick had a fat ass, man," Day-Day shook his head remembering the sight of the stacked young woman.

"Yeah, I know, but that bitch was burning and I wasn't with that shit, condom or no condom. You smell me?" Unique fired up an already-rolled blunt he retrieved from his top pocket.

"No doubt, B, no doubt."

The two young men stood in the doorway of the apartment building, passing the blunt back and forth between them. Unique began to pull knot after knot from the different pockets of his coat. He arranged the loose money, sliding it into the grip he already had neatly in order. He passed Day-Day three bundles to hold.

"What's that right there?" Unique asked.

"That's six yards. I got about two-and-a-half right here."

"Yo, let's bounce. It's five minutes to three," Unique said, looking at his cell phone.

"Aight, hold up," Day-Day said while he continued to put the money in order and place it back in his pockets. "Let me get the stash out the hallway, and we out." He turned and went into the building's hallway.

Unique jumped up and down in an attempt to heat up his body. He poked out his head from the entrance, looking up and down the street. Up the block he could see someone moving toward the building. He watched as the figure moved from side to side in a drunken stupor. He rubbed his hands together and put them to his mouth, blowing warm air into them, never taking his eyes off the character. As the figure came closer, Unique could see it was a man who appeared to be completely inebriated.

The man stood about six foot two inches. He was wearing a wool trench overcoat, a black scully that was pulled down to his eyes, and a winter scarf tied around the lower half of his face, creating a mummy look. A cigarette dangled between his fingers as he stumbled, almost falling to the ground. He landed on a nearby, parked car and rested there for a moment.

Day-Day came through the building's door, holding a brown paper bag. He was rolling up the bag when he noticed his friend was staring at something.

"What's up, man?" he asked.

"Look at this muthafucka right here." Unique pointed toward the drunk.

"Damn, that nigga out on his feet."

They both watched as the man made several attempts to push himself off the car, finally falling to his knees. They laughed as the man had difficulty getting his bearings. Finally he was able to regain his balance and continued to stumble toward the building.

"Yo, you ready?" Unique asked.

"Yeah, let's roll," Day-Day answered.

The two teens stepped down off the step and hunched their shoulders in an attempt to block the oncoming wind. They walked beside each other, heading toward the drunk.

"This muthafucka is twisted," Unique said.

Just as they were about to walk past the drunk, he stumbled and bumped hard into Unique. Unique was then knocked into Day-Day, who fell to the ground.

"Damn, nigga, what the fuck is wrong with yo' drunk ass?" Unique asked.

Day-Day scurried to his feet. "Muthafucka, I should split your skull for that bullshit," he yelled, reaching for the concealed weapon located down the front waistband of his jeans.

Before he could remove his gun, the drunk retrieved a .357 Magnum from inside of his coat and blew a gaping hole through Day-Day's neck. The blast from the cannon sent Day-Day flying into the alley on the side of the building. Unique was in shock and failed to reach for his own weapon before the .357 was then turned on him.

"Run, ya shit," the drunk said with a raspy voice.

"Yo, man, here. Just take the shit and let me live." Unique reached into his pocket and threw the knots to the ground.

The gunman stood there, staring at Unique as if he didn't

believe him. Unique reached into another coat pocket and threw the rolled-up paper bag to the ground. The gunman unloaded a round into Unique's knee, nearly severing the lower leg. Unique fell to the ground, eyes wide in a state of shock. No sound came from his mouth due to the numbing pain. The gunman walked over to Day-Day's dead body and removed the money from his pockets. He turned and walked out from the side of the building while pulling a .40 caliber weapon from the waist of his jeans. Never breaking his stride, he let off two rounds into Unique's head as he stepped over him and proceeded down the street.

CHAPTER 2

Detective Rick Daniels walked into the pool hall where a few scattered people played on several tables. He walked briskly through the dimly-lit establishment as onlookers stared at him, aware that he was the police. He proceeded confidently toward the office door in the rear of the hall, like he'd been there before. As he neared the rear, he was stopped by a big, burly man wearing a tailored, Italian suit just before he reached the office door. Big Dak was Leroy's right hand man and his personal security guard.

"Can I help you with something, officer?" Big Dak asked with his deep voice.

"Yeah, you can step aside and let me handle my business. Police business, that is," he said, looking up at the six-foot-seven, four-hundred-pound man.

Detective Daniels stood six feet even. He was of a dark brown complexion, clean-shaven with a low, cropped haircut. He had deep, dark eyes, a suave personality and a unique swagger to go with his good looks. These characteristics had gotten him more than his share of women throughout his lifetime.

"Who are you looking for? Maybe I can help you."

"I'm not gonna say it again. This is police business. Now step aside." He eyed the man intensely, letting him know he meant business.

Big Dak slowly stepped to the side, never taking his eyes off the cop. Detective Daniels proceeded through the heavy metal door with Big Dak on his heels.

Leroy "Big Roy" Jenkins was in his usual spot behind his desk. He was leaning back, resting comfortably in his high-backed leather chair while smoking a Cuban cigar. He leaned forward in his chair and smiled, not saying a word as Detective Daniels entered his office. He waved his hand at Detective Daniels to come in, as if he was waiting for Leroy to give permission.

Detective Daniels sat in one of the chairs in front of Leroy's desk. A tall, plus-sized Brazilian woman walked over to Detective Daniels. He looked up at the woman, wondering what she wanted.

"Drink?" Leroy offered him.

"No," Detective Daniels said, staring at the voluptuous beauty.

Leroy waved his hand to dismiss Big Dak and the woman from the office.

"How's it going, Rick?" Leroy asked as he leaned back in his chair. Clouds of smoke circled his face, creating a smokescreen illusion.

"Same ol', same ol'." Detective Daniels shrugged. "So what's the deal with Ishmael's murder?"

"Shit, Rick, I don't have a clue. I mean, killing Ishmael hit close to home for me," Leroy stated with concern on his face.

"I bet it does. Who do you think did it?"

"Hell, it could be anybody. You know Ishmael had street status so any jealous punk could have done it. All I know is Ishmael wasn't no easy nigga to get next to." Leroy puffed on his cigar and continued to play his part as if he was clueless about the murder.

Leroy had nothing but love for Ishmael. It was a mistake that his men had killed him and it hurt him to his heart. But, Leroy has seen it all and over the years, conditioned himself to handle those types of situations. As far as he was concerned, life still goes on and business could not run on emotions.

"Well, he obviously got caught slippin'. Captain Cohen and several other people were murdered during the same night. I'm all over this case. Trust me, I will find out."

"Yeah? Well, I hope you get what you're looking for." Leroy eyed the detective putting up a front.

Detective Daniels crossed his legs and leaned back in the chair tired of the bullshit game play with Leroy.

"So who you gonna get to distribute your product for your frontin' ass now, Leroy?"

Leroy shook his head and bellowed out a hearty laugh.

"I'm an entrepreneur, Rick. You know that. I run several legitimate and prestigious businesses—"

"You mean your businesses are the front for what you really do," Detective Daniels interrupted. Leroy continued without hesitation.

"Rick, I'm a lover, not a fighter. You're not talking to one of them punks from off the streets. Didn't your mother teach you to respect your elders?" Leroy asked as he frowned.

"You're mighty defensive, Leroy. Should I be suspecting that you may know more than you're telling me?"

"Fuck is you trying to say, Rick?" Leroy asked, laughing.

"I think I already said it. Listen, Leroy, I ain't new to this. I'm true to this. Now we talkin' about murder on my streets. I need you down at the precinct ASAP." Detective Daniels stood.

"Come on, Rick. You're reaching, man. I was questioned several months ago. If they haven't found the killer yet, then maybe you should let it go, too. I've answered all the questions I'm prepared to answer," Leroy stated, twirling the cigar in his mouth.

"I've been assigned to this cold case and I'm a man who gets the job done. You can bet your balls on that one, Leroy."

"Got you a little promotion to detective and you Billy Bad Ass now, huh?" Leroy bellowed out another laugh. Both men stared at each other.

"Don't let me have to issue a warrant for your arrest, Leroy, because it ain't a thing for me to do that."

Leroy stared at Detective Daniels with one eye, squinting from the smoke of the cigar.

"Sure, Rick, I'll see you first thing in the morning."

"Make that nine in the morning, Leroy." Detective Daniels turned and began walking toward the door.

"You gotta have your coffee and donuts first, huh, Rick?"

Detective Daniels never broke stride as he continued through the door while the echo of Leroy's laughter followed him.

Detective Daniels had been promoted to lead detective for the precinct after Captain Cohen was killed and operation D.T.E.F. (Drug Enforcement Task Force) had been shut down. He sat in the back for years and watched the other detectives scramble around, trying to take down dealers of the drug-infested city. He always felt that if given the opportunity, he would do a much better job. He had come a long way from the beat cop that he was when he and his partner patrolled the streets on foot. Those days were over, but since then he had acquired a certain amount of respect from the good citizens that were forced to live in the hood.

Detective Daniels had several ideas and suspicions about the murders that took place several months ago, with Leroy being his main suspect. With his sharp instinct and the hunger for the job dwelling in his body, he knew that, in a matter of time, he would take down his perp.

"What was that all about, Roy?" Big Dak asked after Detective Daniels had left.

"Cocksucker says he wants me to come down to the station for questioning."

"I thought you been through questioning already?"

"Yeah, I have. I see this nigga wants to make a name for himself by brown-nosing his way to the top. Get me Tony's number," Leroy said, referring to the former mayor.

"Sure, Roy." The big man quickly left the room.

Detective Daniels sat at a red light in his unmarked Ford Explorer, his mind preoccupied with the case. His radio hissed and static blasted from it.

"Car two-two-seven," the radio dispatcher announced.

"Two-two-seven," Detective Daniels said into the radio.

"Car two-two-seven, one eighty-seven at Isabella and Eighteenth Avenues - Code two. EMTs and units already on the scene." The static echoed from the radio.

"Two-two-seven, roger that. Shit!" Detective Daniels threw on his lights and sirens and proceeded through the red light.

CHAPTER 3

"Yo, TJ man, why you always so quiet?" a young boy named Tyler asked.

TJ simply shrugged his shoulders as he sat there on the porch with his head held low.

The sun was shining brightly but brought minimal heat to the chilly mid-morning air. Tyler lived next door to TJ and seemed to be the only kid who would hang around him. Tyler was thirteen-years-old and not very popular, due to the fact that his mother was strict and kept a tight leash on him. Because of her own past, she didn't want her only living son to be swallowed up by the streets as they had done to her brother, sister and almost herself.

TJ had just turned twelve, but his height and demeanor made him look as if he were fifteen. He stood at five feet ten inches with a lean, muscular body and a handsome face with peach fuzz growing on top of his lip. He and his sister had moved in with their grandmother several months ago after their mother had been murdered. They were transported off to Child Protective Services until their grandmother, at the age of sixty-seven, came to rescue them. TJ's grandmother was, most times, physically unable to take care of herself because she had arthritis, diabetes, and high blood pressure. At her age she needed the kids to help her out. She was too old to chase behind them but she prayed every night that they would not turn out like their mother or her other children that had since died.

Since the death of his mother, TJ had become distant and didn't communicate well with others. He kept to himself and appeared to be a very reserved and serious boy. After he moved in with his grandmother, he barely attended school. On most days he sat on the porch or in the basement of the three-story home. Although he barely talked to Tyler, TJ did like his company.

Two police cars with sirens blaring raced up the block, passing the house where the two boys sat on the porch. They heard more sirens in the distance. Both boys stood to their feet to get a better look and realized the action was down the street, on the corner.

"Hey, TJ, let's go down there, man, and see what happened."

"You can go," TJ said, sitting back down.

"Come on. We can just go halfway and maybe we can see something. I know somebody probably got smoked because the ambulance is down there, too," Tyler said excitedly.

Tyler was fascinated by the action that took place on the streets. He would sit in his bedroom window at night, at the front of the building, and watch the drug users walk past on their way down to the corner to purchase. Sometimes Tyler would sneak out of the house and walk down the long block, close enough to see actual drug transactions. It really excited him to see how dominant and powerful the young dealers were. All he ever wanted was to be liked and popular.

TJ, on the other hand, could care less about what was going on down at the main intersection corners. Although his mother was now gone and they hadn't had the closest relationship, he still missed her dearly. She had taken good care of his sister and him, regardless of her crutch.

Tyler had stepped down onto the sidewalk and stood there looking up at TJ, waiting for an answer. TJ looked up at his friend, seeing that he desperately wanted to go, so TJ reluctantly stood.

The two boys began the walk down the street. Tyler went on and on, wondering whether there was a bloody body at the corner. He wanted to see someone being put into the ambulance with their guts hanging out. TJ just looked at his friend and shook his head.

"You watch too much TV, man," TJ said quietly.

"Yeah, but some of that stuff is for real on TV. Where do you think they get the stories from? They get them from real people. Like *New Jack City*, there had to be a real Nino Brown. Man, if I had the kind of status Nino Brown had, I would be on top of the world. . . ." Tyler continued to ramble on as they walked down the block.

As the two got closer Tyler stopped talking and began to walk a little faster, completely forgetting that he had asked TJ to go halfway with him. TJ continued to follow his friend, realizing that he needed to protect Tyler from his naiveté.

A crowd had gathered in front of the five-story apartment building on the corner. Tyler squeezed his way through the crowd, trying to get a front-row seat. TJ followed behind him, observing the faces that stood around. He knew most of the drug addicts that stood there, looking at the scene.

Once TJ stepped to the forefront, he just stared at the two bodies that lay there. One of the bodies lay in the alley next to the building. He had never seen a hole so big on a human body in his life. He actually wondered how the head was still in place.

"TJ, look at that cat's knee. I told you somebody probably got smoked," Tyler said excitedly.

As TJ stood there, staring at the two bodies, images of his mother's funeral jumped into his head. He had nightmares night after night, thinking about finding his mother's killer. When he looked up from the boy's body, he locked eyes with one of the plainclothes police officers. He didn't look like a cop, but TJ knew he was. The stare was intense and made him uncomfortable. The cop finally broke the stare and kept walking. TJ turned swiftly and pushed his way through the crowd, marching back up the street toward his home.

"Hey, TJ, what's wrong, man?" Tyler ran after him.

"Nothing." He kept walking.

"Well, why did you leave?"

"They're dead. What do you want to look at dead bodies for?" TJ asked with exasperation written all over his face.

"What's really wrong, TJ?" Tyler grabbed his arm to stop him.

TJ looked at the ground with his hands shoved into his jean pockets. He shrugged his shoulders and kicked a can that lay near the curb.

"It's me, isn't it? No one likes me and now you don't even like me," Tyler stated with a look of defeat.

"C'mon, it's not you. It's me. Let's go play X-box in my room," TJ said in an attempt to change the subject and cheer up his friend. The two walked back up the street, shoulder to shoulder.

CHAPTER 4

Detective Daniels pulled onto Eighteenth Ave. and parked his vehicle behind the other cruisers that were double-parked. The traffic was being redirected by two uniformed policemen. He hopped out of his vehicle, leaving the police lights flashing and he made his way through the crowd of pedestrians standing around, trying to see what happened.

"Excuse me." He brushed past a woman. "Let's get these people back!"

Several officers began to move the bystanders back and away from the scene.

"Why the hell isn't there any police tape roping off the scene?" he asked no one in particular. "Jesus!" He continued to push forward toward the scene.

Investigator David Blist was kneeling down beside one of the bodies. He looked up to see Detective Daniels headed his way. Blist stood and began writing in a note pad he was holding.

Investigator Blist was from the old school. He was a reserved man and had seen it all in the fifty-five years of his life. Unlike Detective Daniels or any of the other young detectives, he took the job with a grain of salt and with two years left to serve, was cruising toward his retirement. Each day he dreamed of sitting on his fifty-foot, Sirocco power boat, casting his line into the water. He often laughed as he watched detectives like Daniels; they were so hyper and hungry, not giving any thought to the job they would be doing for the next twenty years.

"What do we have here? Robbery?" Detective Daniels squatted down beside the teen's body and tilted his head to the side to get a better look at the two bullet holes lodged into his head. One bullet had entered into the middle of the forehead and the second went into the right eye, leaving a gaping hole.

"I doubt it, because they're still sporting their jewelry. Could be a drug rivalry. These guys could have been on the wrong side of the tracks, selling dope. Who knows nowadays," Blist stated. "Come over here, Rick." He waved.

As Detective Daniels stood to walk away, he noticed that the deceased male's knee was blown open. He shook his head and continued the walk. He observed the onlookers standing by and he locked eyes with a young boy in the crowd. The boy quickly lowered his head and Detective Daniels kept walking. As he entered the alley, he could see another male teenager lying on his back. It appeared that his neck was broken. Once he got closer he saw the cause of the teen's crooked neck.

"Shit, what the hell happened to him? Looks like a double-barreled shotgun wound." Detective Daniels's face showed disgust.

"More like a World War II cannon." Blist got a closer

look at the wound.

"All right. Wait for the crime lab to get here. In the meantime, are there any witnesses?" Detective Daniels asked. Blist looked up at Detective Daniels like he was crazy.

"You know the code of the street."

"Yeah, yeah, that's bullshit. Somebody knows something and I'm gonna find out." Detective Daniels walked back out to the sidewalk just as the crime scene investigation crew arrived. Some of the pedestrians had left the scene and the crowd looked thinner than when he first arrived. Detective Daniels walked over to his vehicle and grabbed his cigarettes, which sat on the dashboard. After lighting one of the cancer sticks, he shut the door and leaned on the truck. He watched as Blist made his way through the crowd, heading in his direction.

"So what's on your mind?" Blist joined him, leaning against the truck.

"I need you to find out who those two kids run with," he said, blowing smoke from his nose.

"Who are you thinking they worked for?"

"I don't know, but if I find out that has-been Leroy Jenkins has his scent on these boys' bodies, I'ma be all over his ass like stink on shit." He tossed the barely-smoked cigarette to the ground. "Get at me when you find out anything. I'm gonna go talk to some people that might know something about this."

He opened the door to the truck and hopped in.

"What about your CI?" Blist asked, stepping up to the driver's side window.

"That's the first person I'm gonna go see." Detective Daniels started the ignition and pulled off.

-❖-❖-❖-

Detective Daniels drove at a slow pace. He watched as the dealers alerted one another to his presence. He kept a watchful eye on their body language and behavior. Although they knew he was police and warned the others, he still needed to stay on top of his game. The young kids in the school of hard knocks today were heartless and fearless. At any given moment, they wouldn't hesitate to kill an officer of the law.

Drug fiends stood around or walked away as he continued down the street. Leaning up against a building, a man stood and watched as Detective Daniels drove past. They both looked into each other's eyes and then Detective Daniels sped off. He circled the block and pulled into the driveway of an abandoned house. Several minutes later, the man leaning up against the building stepped into the driveway and got into the backseat of the truck.

"What's up, man?" Detective Daniels asked, turning around to face him.

"Hey, what's going on, brother?" the man asked, looking around to make sure no one had spotted him get into the vehicle.

The windows of Detective Daniels's police truck were covered with limousine tint, but this still did nothing to help the man's nervous behavior. This was the natural behavior for a snitch. The man scooted down in the seat and looked at Detective Daniels.

"What you need, man?" he asked Detective Daniels.

"I need some information. What's the word on the

street about the two kids that got burnt over on Isabella and Eighteenth?"

"Man, ain't nobody really saying nothing. Don't nobody really know who did it."

"So you tryna tell me that nobody is talking at all?" Detective Daniels gave him a look of disbelief.

"Yeah, man, I'm dead-ass serious. You know if I knew something, I would tell you." The man wiped his running nose with the back of his coat sleeve.

Detective Daniels stared at him for a moment.

"All right, if you hear anything, get in touch with me. I'll be coming back through here in a week."

"Yeah, a'ight. You gonna throw me a bone?" he asked.

Detective Daniels hesitated at first, then reached into his pocket and pulled out a ten-dollar bill and handed it to the man over the seat. The man looked at the money and then back up at Detective Daniels.

"What? You ain't give up no info, homeboy. How can you be an informant with no information, and still expect to get paid? Man, you better raise up outta my truck," Detective Daniels warned.

The derelict man looked around nervously before he eased the back door open and slipped out of the truck. He ran through the backyard of the abandoned house instead of going out the same way he had arrived.

CHAPTER 5

The night air was warm and breezy. Darkness covered the woods with the exception of light from a full mass moon, which sent moonbeams through the tall trees. Owls and other night creatures made loud noises, simultaneously creating an eerie atmosphere.

Quick-moving footsteps pounded through the wooded area. Twigs and sticks crunched underfoot with each step. Short and hard breaths emitted from the woman who ran, deeply sucking in night air as she attempted to catch her breath. Distress covered her face as she looked back at her pursuers. The two of them closing in on her as the others trailed behind. She tried to pick up her pace, but the pain in her side was a reminder of how physically out of shape she was.

She forced herself to bear down and deal with the pain, pushing herself a little harder with each step. She swung her elbows as fast as she could in an attempt to move faster while jumping over logs and dodging low branches. She turned to look behind her once again and her pursuers were within arm's reach. Fear took over her body. She was finally able to see the faces of the two culprits giving chase. The hunters, a male and a female, almost looked to be gliding rather than running. Their faces were distorted, their eyes bulged out of their heads and they both held large switchblade razors in their hands. The grimace plastered across their cracked, bloody lips caused chills to run up the woman's back. She screamed loudly, releasing fear through her vocal chords.

"Get away from me!"

Up ahead she could see light, someone to help her she thought, as rescue seemed not too far away. Then she heard it—the noise of their blades swinging at her. She could feel the breeze and heard the sweeping sounds of the blades that missed her head by mere inches. A dark shadow walked into the light, in front of her. It appeared to be a man, but the closer she got, the shorter the figure became.

"Run, little boy! Go!" She realized it was a child. She could barely move her legs as fatigue engulfed her body.

She turned to look behind her, no longer hearing her assailants' footfalls. They had vanished. She slowed her pace and began to look around frantically for the pursuers. Her legs felt like rubber and the pain in her chest was unbearable. She fell to her knees just a few feet in front of the young boy. He stood there, innocence covering his face. He was about four-years-old, and he held a Matchbox car in his little hands. His resemblance to Ishmael was remarkable, but he had green eyes like Desiree.

"What are you doing out here?" she asked, barely able to breathe.

The young boy simply smiled and giggled playfully. He pointed his finger past her head. She followed his finger just in time to move out of the way of the switchblade swinging down at her face. She scrambled to her feet to face her attackers as they stepped into the light.

"No!" She began to back up, slipping in the forest rubble.

She was suddenly stopped by a sharp pain in her back from a cut by a razor. She flailed around to meet yet two more zombie-like stalkers. The female's head was partially decapitated and the deep gash exposed dried blood, arteries, and bile. The head wobbled unsteadily on top of the woman's shoulders. The male zombie had a head full of matted, blood-soaked dreads. Blood ran from his eyes and he wore a grimace on his face.

She stumbled, backing away from the zombies, when she bumped into something. She turned to see the first two stalkers that had been chasing her just minutes ago. Again, she screamed. The little boy began to laugh.

"Get her, Daddy!" he yelled.

"No!" she screamed, trying to back away, but she was surrounded by the zombies that looked like Ishmael, Desiree, Beverly, and Derrick.

The switchblade came down on the side of her face, leaving a gaping, two-inch gash. The exposed white meat became flushed red as blood poured from the open wound. The woman felt dizzy and tried to run when another blade caught her across the back of her head. She felt the wind as it blew into her opened skull. She fell to her hands and knees in front of the little boy, who was no longer smiling. His little eyes had turned from green to neon red as they glowed in the dark. He, too, held a switchblade in his tiny hands. He raised the blade high above his head with both hands and came down.

Nettie jumped to her feet, awakening from her nightmare and began to scream.

CHAPTER 6

Nettie stood in the middle of the bed, sweating like a pig on a hot summer's day. A wife beater and woman's boxers stuck to her body like glue. Her eyes bulged out of her head as she whipped her head from side to side, looking around the room, breathing hard. Nettie was frantic. She was looking for the zombies that she dreamed about, the zombies that had been slashing her body to pieces, right before she woke up. When she realized it was yet another nightmare, she dropped down onto the bed and put her head into her hands.

The Spanish beauty that was lying next to Nettie sound asleep, now stood on the side of the bed, looking at Nettie with frustration written on her face. Nettie didn't seem to realize that the beauty was no longer in bed with her.

Nettie looked over to the night table and saw the blade that she usually carried in her mouth and chills ran up her spine. The very blade that Nettie carried for many years of her life was now haunting her in her sleep.

The Spanish beauty cleared her throat, startling Nettie.

"Why are you sneaking up on me?" Nettie yelled at her.

"Sneaking up on you? Coño, you got to be kidding me, Netta," she said in a heavy Spanish accent.

The Spanish beauty's name was Maria and she was a stripper at the same club where Nettie used to dance. They became cool when Nettie started dancing there five years ago. Maria was tough and didn't take no shit from the girls who were jealous of her when she first came to the club. Nettie loved aggressive women. That's why she'd adored Zola, because of her passive/aggressiveness. She knew when to be submissive. Zola was Nettie's past lover and best friend. Nettie believed she was murdered by Ishmael's girlfriend, at the time, Desiree. Back then, Zola and Ishmael had been what they called 'the hottest street couple. That was, until Desiree walked into the picture and snatched him right from under Zola's nose. Nettie despised Ishmael and thought if Zola had listened to her and got rid of him, she'd still be living today.

Nettie was turned on by Maria's beauty, but also by her feistiness. They became friends with benefits, and that included being sexual partners at times.

Maria stood five feet seven inches with jet black, curly, shoulder-length hair. Her skin was golden bronze and looked tanned at all times. She had gray eyes and full lips. Her body was shaped like a goddess and thick in all the right places.

"Netta, I'm so tired of you having these nightmares, no? I can't take it anymore. What is wrong with you, mamí?" She asked as the morning sunlight seeping through the blinds bounced off of her skin.

"I don't know what's wrong," Nettie said, lying down.

"So, was it Desiree again?" Maria asked, climbing into bed. She sat Indian style, wearing lace panties and a body shirt with spaghetti straps. She took off the rubber band, which held her mane together, letting her beautiful hair flow down around her face and shoulders. Maria knew all too well about Nettie's recurring nightmares. They would always be about Derrick or Desiree.

After Zola was murdered, Nettie and Maria became even closer. She confided in Maria on what took place that night. Nettie decided to quit dancing and lay low for a while after Maria suggested it. Maria felt that if Nettie was not in the spotlight so much, then there wouldn't be a chance of her being blamed for the murders of Ishmael, Desiree, Derrick and Beverly. Especially since most people knew she carried a blade in her mouth and wouldn't hesitate to use it. Some on the streets really believed that Nettie had something to do with Beverly's and Desiree's deaths at the cemetery, because of their necks being slit. But no one said a word. Maria took Nettie in and put in more hours at the club to make ends meet.

"OK, mamí, so what we gonna do about this situation, huh?" Maria asked.

"Maria, I was thinking. I got a plan that I think may bring us a lot of money," Nettie said, ignoring Maria's question. "I been thinking about this for a long time and all I need to do is put a team together and set it off. I just know it will work."

"What plan?"

"The plan to make some money," Nettie repeated.

"OK, you know what? I'm talking to you about these

crazy dreams and you sitting here talking about money." Maria rocked her head from side to side with each word as her accent thickened. "So what are we going to do about that, huh?"

"Maria, I don't want to talk about that now. Let me tell you about my plan." Nettie blew her off.

Maria blew air through her nose. "Okay, so what you talking, mamí?"

Nettie sat up on the bed and began to run down the plan to Maria and she listened intently without saying a word. Nettie told her she was going to have to put in work and it was going to be dangerous and risky for both of them. Nettie also knew that they needed to get a dependable and reliable crew together to help execute the plan. They could lose their lives if they tried to do it alone and Nettie knew that it would take careful handpicking of crew members.

Nettie placed her hand to her forehead and began to rub it, feeling the beginning of a headache coming on. Maria was silent and sat staring at her.

"I think I'm gonna go over to my mother's house for a visit," Nettie said.

"Your Madre's house? I thought you hated going over there, Netta?" Maria asked, puzzled.

"I do, but I need to see my niece and nephew. I haven't seen them in a long time. I just feel the need to see them because I do miss and love them." She didn't say why she really needed to go to her mother's house.

"But you said you would never go over there again. You said you couldn't stand your sister and your mother, Netta." Maria's accent thickened again.

"I know what I said, Maria. Stop sweating me. I said I was going to see my niece and nephew." Nettie lay on her side, facing Maria.

"So what about the baby?"

"What about the baby?" Nettie mean-mugged Maria.

"Forget it," Maria said, lowering her head. She knew that was a touchy subject. At times Maria wanted to talk about the baby, but Nettie would never say anything other than what she had already told Maria.

"Listen, Maria, you gotta trust that everything I do is for us. I'm gonna do some things you may not agree with, and be with people you may not like, but always remember it's for us. You feel me?"

Maria looked into Nettie's eyes and nodded her head in agreement.

"Are you game?" Nettie asked Maria.

"Sí, mamí, I'm game. Somos hermana para la vida. Chicas forever, mamí!"

"Sisters for life, huh?" Nettie knew what Maria had just said. It wasn't the first time Maria has said that to her. "I hope you mean that, Maria."

"Sí, mamí, I do, but I hope you're ready for what you're about to start, Netta," Maria said seriously.

Nettie looked into Maria's gorgeous gray eyes. Then she looked down at Maria's erect nipples that protruded through her tight shirt.

"Sí, ma, I'm ready," Nettie said, grabbing her arm and pulling Maria down on top of her.

CHAPTER 7

Detective Daniels had been driving around for an hour, speaking to various people, and still he was no wiser than when he first arrived on the scene. His cell phone rang and he looked at the incoming call.

"Hey, beautiful," he said into the receiver.

"Hey yourself," the woman responded.

"What are you doing?"

"Well, I was wondering why I haven't heard from you all day, and I decided to give you a call," she said.

"Well, you know how police work is, baby. Sometimes it's busy and sometimes it's not. Today happens to be one of those busy days." He smiled as he held the phone and drove his truck with one hand.

"I know. Do you think you can come by and see me right quick?" she asked.

"For sure. I'll be there in ten minutes."

"OK, see you then. Bye, bye." She hung up the phone.

Ten minutes later Detective Daniels pulled up in front of a two-family house. Before he could shut off the engine the woman was coming from inside the house. She skipped down the stairs and over to the truck. Once inside, she leaned over and gave him a passionate kiss. Their tongues danced a waltz together in total bliss. Their bodies began to heat up quickly, since their last sexual encounter was two weeks ago due to Detective Daniels's tight schedule.

"I miss you so much, baby," she panted as he planted wet kisses on her neck.

She placed her hand between his legs until she found his growing erection. She began to massage the shaft up and down. Detective Daniels rubbed her breasts and placed his hand inside her bra, removing her breasts from it. He then began to suck on her nipples while she moaned lightly from the pleasure he was giving.

"Hold on, babe," she panted. "We gotta stop doing this right here."

"What?" he asked, breathing hard and still holding a breast in his hand.

"I mean, look at us, acting like we're some high school kids, getting busy in the car. We're too old for this. When are you going to have time for me?"

Detective Daniels sat back in his seat and rubbed his forehead.

"Come on, Janet. How many times do we have to go through this?" He looked at her. "How many times do I have to keep explaining that to you?"

"Try one more time because obviously I'm not getting it." She put her breasts back in the bra and folded her arms across her chest, pouting like a child.

"Listen, you knew what came with the job when I met you. I talked to you about this in the beginning. I was honest with you, Janet. You knew that my time would be limited, especially when I have an investigation that I need to close. Janet, don't act like this is all new to you. You didn't seem to have a problem with it when you was . . ." He trailed off after noticing her facial expression.

"No, Rick, don't stop. Go ahead and say it. When I was locked up, right? That's what you want to say, isn't it? I knew you would eventually use that against me. You're just like everybody else. And don't get it twisted: When I met you, you weren't a detective. You was a beat cop!" She turned to look out the window.

Detective Daniels felt bad. He didn't mean for it to come out the way that it did, but he was growing weary of her complaining. He really cared for Janet, but his job would always be a priority in his life. He had worked hard to get promoted to detective.

"Janet, baby, I'm sorry. I didn't mean for it to come out that way. But, baby, in the beginning you said you understood."

"That was before I fell in love with you, Rick. I know how important the job is to you. But you are not even trying to spend time with me anymore. I mean, I am not proud of the things I did in the past, and I think I have paid for the mistakes I've made. The last thing I need from you is the constant reminder." She was pissed with him.

"I know, baby, I know. How about I come pick you up, say around ten tonight, and we can go get something to eat from the diner? That's about the best I can do with the schedule that I have right now. I've got two murders that I need to solve and a bunch of other open case files. I just don't have the time right now."

"You know it's the same story all the time. At least I can say you're consistent," she said.

Detective Daniels just continued to look at her. He then leaned over and began kissing her on the neck. "Come on, baby, don't be like that."

"Am I just a car booty call to you, Rick?" she asked, leaning away from him and looking into his face.

"Huh? What did you say?"

"I don't think I stutter when I talk. If you can 'huh,' you can hear."

"I don't need this right now, Janet, especially not from you. No, you're not a booty call. I don't know what else to tell you, baby. It is what it is. My job demands my time." He grabbed her hand. "I care about you, Janet, and I promise it won't always be like this. Just be patient with me and you'll see." He kissed the back of her hand.

"All right, call me when you're on the way and I'll be ready. I do understand your job, Rick, but I also noticed that you've been neglecting me as well. If I don't call you, you won't call me. I'll see you later." She leaned over, gave him a peck on the lips and got out of the car without saying another word.

Detective Daniels knew Janet really didn't understand. He watched her go into the house and started his truck before pulling off.

CHAPTER 8

Hours later.

Although the weather was cold, children still played in the street. Music blared from a car's woofer speakers as the owner concentrated on painting *Armor All* on the tires. Nettie parked her BMW in the driveway of a two-family home. She killed the engine and got out of the car.

As she climbed the stairs, the screen door of the house came flying open. An eight-year-old little girl ran into her arms.

"Auntie Nettie!" the little girl screamed.

"Hey, pumpkin, how are you?"

"I'm fine." She smiled up at her.

"C'mon, let's get out of the cold," Nettie said

"Where have you been?" she asked.

"I've been around," Nettie said, grabbing the girl's hand and leading her back into the house.

"Nah-uh, you been gone a long, *long* time."

"Naeesha, it has not been that long. Stop exaggerating."

"What's zaggerate?" Naeesha asked innocently.

Nettie laughed, bent down and kissed her niece on the forehead.

"Where's Tyler?" Nettie asked.

"He's next door with his friend TJ."

Nettie was at her mother, Carolyn's, house. Although their relationship was not the best, she still felt the need to visit with her niece and nephew. Just to see their bright faces melted her icy heart. Nettie had a sister and an older brother. Their mother had Nettie and her sister late in life by her third husband, who had been twenty years younger. Carolyn was pushing seventy and she looked good for her age. Although she was still very much a feisty woman, she was handicapped and bound to a wheelchair. Carolyn had to have her legs amputated from the knees down, due to a bad infection. Nettie's sister, Janet, had been locked up at the time and had to leave her children with Carolyn. When she got out, she came to live there and assist with her mother's care.

"Who is that?" Carolyn yelled from the living room.

"It's me, Ma." Nettie could tell she was in a mood, which meant her plan for coming over, flew right out the window.

"Yeah, Nana, it's Auntie," Naeesha co-signed.

Nettie entered the living room still holding Naeesha's hand. She walked over to her mother and kissed her on the cheek. She then looked over at the coffee table and smiled at the little boy that sat in a walker. He returned a toothless smile as his green eyes lit up.

"Hey, little man," she said to the baby as she removed her coat.

The little boy wobbled and shoved his hand in his mouth as saliva ran down his arm.

"When are you coming to get this boy? I can't take care of him in a wheelchair and I'm too old for this."

"I know, Ma. As soon as I get my own place and a stable job, I'm coming to get him."

"I don't understand how you just lay up and have a baby and don't nobody know you had one. Then you just show up here with the child and leave him on me. That ain't right, Jeanette Wright," Carolyn stated, calling Nettie by her birth name.

"C'mon, Ma, let's not do this again." Nettie picked up the baby and sat down on the sofa.

"Let's not do this again? You must think I'm some kinda fool. I wasn't born yesterday, Jeanette. You never came here to see me and then you showed up here with a baby, telling me a bullshit story and expecting me to accept it. No! Hell no, Jeanette!" Carolyn was heated.

"Ooh, Nana, you cursed," Naeesha said, holding the baby's hand as she sat next to Nettie.

"Go play somewhere, Naeesha, with your grown self," Carolyn demanded.

"Go 'head, Naeesha. I'm not leaving yet," Nettie assured her.

Naeesha skipped out of the living room, unfazed by the scolding. Carolyn turned her electric wheelchair around and rolled over to the couch.

"Where's the child's paperwork, Jeanette?"

Nettie rolled her eyes and laid her head onto the back of the sofa.

"Ma, I told you, it got lost in the fire. I have to go downtown and get more copies."

"Listen to me. I don't know what you're into, but I don't like it. None of this makes sense to me. Where is the child's father? What's he doing? Why isn't he involved with this baby? Why didn't you take this child to his family? I can't afford to take care of this child and you ain't giving me any money to help me." Lines of exhaustion embedded themselves in Carolyn's forehead as she spoke.

"What's with the twenty questions, Ma? I told you that as soon as I get on my feet, I would come and get the baby."

"Well, when are you going to do that?" a female voice interrupted.

Nettie and Carolyn both turned to see Janet standing in the living room doorway, scowling at Nettie. It was no secret that there was no love between the two of them. They both stared at each other with hatred written all over their faces.

"You know, it seems to me that you tryin' to play Mommy by dropping your load on her. I don't think you have any intention to come and get this baby at all."

She walked into the living room. Janet was as pretty as Nettie, with the same body build, except Janet was a little thicker in the breasts. Her hair was even almost the same length, but Janet wore her hair in a neat ponytail most of the time.

The baby began to make playful noises as he bounced up and down on Nettie's lap, unaware of the tension that was quickly building in the room.

"I know you ain't talking. You living up in here with your two kids, freeloading off of Ma."

"Freeloading? I'm the one that's here taking care of Mommy, my kids, and that sperm donor's baby you brought through here. So don't get it twisted, boo-boo. I'm not the freeloader."

Nettie stood and walked over to the walker, placing the giggling baby down in it. She then turned around and placed her hand on her hips.

"What you need to do is raise up outta my face and get you a man. Don't hate on me because I still got it going on," she said, running her hands along her hips, outlining her perfectly shaped body.

"Trick, please, you a stripper! You running around here, doing tricks for a treat. You probably don't know who the father of that baby is." Janet rolled her eyes.

"I don't dance anymore—" Nettie barely got the words out of her mouth.

"Stop it right now!" Carolyn yelled. "I am so sick of the two of you. When does the hatred stop? You two use to be so close. You use to be inseparable. You were like Frick and Frack. What happened?" Carolyn asked, clearly showing hurt for her daughter's bitterness toward each other.

Both sisters continued to stare at each other with piercing eyes, knowing why they'd become the way they were now. It was true that the two of them were once the best of friends, as well as sisters. They did everything together. If one was punished, the other took the punishment with her so that they would be together. If one of them got whipped, the other cried for her. But then it all came to an abrupt end and they became bitter enemies a few years ago.

As they stood there, mean mugging each other, Carolyn became weary. A lone tear raced down her cheek while her stubborn daughters refused to explain their behavior of the past few years.

"What's going on in here?" The question came from a man who looked to be in his late fifties.

Everyone turned around to see Nettie and Janet's older brother, James, standing in the doorway, looking a total mess. No one had even heard him come into the house.

"What are you doing here, James?" Janet asked with anger still written on her face.

"Hey, Nettie. How you doing?" James said after he looked over and noticed her standing there. He ignored Janet as he usually did.

"What's up, Jay?" Nettie asked.

"Hey, James, baby, you okay? Are you hungry?" Carolyn asked, looking at her only son and eldest child. She felt sorry for him and still treated him like a child.

"Mommy, he is not a child and I told him I didn't want him here anymore. I'm surprised I didn't smell him come in." Janet rolled her eyes at him. James just laughed at her.

"That's all you got, Janet? I know you can come better than that. You still kickin' dirt on a man when he down."

"Kicking dirt on a man? Show me a real man, because it sure ain't you. Hell, you like rolling around in dirt." She rolled her eyes at him.

James waved his hand at Janet in dismissal and went over to his mother and kissed her.

"How you feeling today, Ma?"

"I'm good, baby, but you could use a bath. Why don't you go on upstairs and take a shower?" Carolyn asked, turning up her nose.

"Later, Ma. Right now I need to talk to you." James got behind the wheelchair and started to push Carolyn out of the room when Janet intervened.

"Oh hell no, James! Anything you got to say to Mommy, you can say right here."

"This ain't none of your business, Janet." He looked at her seriously.

"I don't give a flying fuck! Mommy *is* my business. Neither one of y'all's sorry asses help me do shit, so get ya dirty hands off her chair," Janet yelled.

Carolyn just put her head in her hands and shook her head. Her family had fallen apart years ago, but she was too old and to tired to deal with the constant bickering.

"Who you calling sorry?" Nettie asked.

"You!"

Nettie and Janet began to argue again. James bent down and began to whisper in Carolyn's ear.

James was an addict and had been for well over twenty years. Although he had the addiction, he was still a very good man at heart. Janet, however, couldn't and didn't want to see that. She refused to acknowledge him as her brother. James had stolen from the house on many occasions and Janet had banned him from coming there. He'd talked their mother into giving him money from her social security check on countless occasions.

Janet realized that Carolyn was going into her bra to get her money.

"Don't give him no money, Ma," she yelled.

"Janet, you treat me like a stranger," James said.

"Janet, he just needs twenty dollars to get a haircut," Carolyn said, trying to reason.

"Mommy! You can't be serious? Ain't no barber in the country gonna put him in their chair to cut his hair. Stop playin'! He gonna buy drugs with the money, Ma!" Janet was steaming.

"Damn, Janet, I'm ya brother."

"No, my brother died a long time ago. Now, get out before I call the cops." She pointed toward the door.

"Janet, the least we could do is give him something to eat." Carolyn tried to reason again.

"No!" Janet said firmly.

James looked to his mother and Nettie for help.

"You better go, baby," Carolyn told him.

Defeated, he dropped his head and walked toward the door with Janet on his heels, making sure he didn't lift anything on the way out.

CHAPTER 9

"Jay, c'mere," Nettie called out to James as she stepped onto the porch.

James was standing several houses away talking to one of the neighbors when Nettie called to him. He turned and began walking back toward the house.

James stood about five feet nine inches. His skin was dark, due to his years of drug use and lack of hygiene. His face sported a full beard that was matted and filled with lint. Some called him Black Santa, due to the overgrowth of hairs on his face. Given the opportunity to clean up, James would be a strictly handsome man as he had once been.

Nettie walked down the steps to meet him as he walked toward her.

"Janet ain't right, Nettie," he said.

"I know. Don't let that psycho bitch get in ya head, Jay."

"I know what I am and I'm not proud of it. I'ma forty-nine-year-old man walking 'round here, not knowing where my next meal is gonna come from. I don't know where I'ma sleep and sometimes if I'm gonna even wake up. I've tried to kick this thing, Nettie, but it ain't easy. How do you think I feel?"

The eyes never lie and you could see the sincerity and a cry for help in James' eyes.

When the wind shifted, it blew his body odor in Nettie's direction, sending a sickening feeling into the pit of her stomach.

"Look, I hear you, but you said it yourself. You've been using for too many years. Why don't you get some help?" She rubbed the bottom of her nostrils with her finger in an attempt to block the horrible smell from entering her nose.

"I tried, Nettie. Were you listening? It ain't easy . . ."

In fact, Nettie was not listening to what her brother was saying. While James talked, Nettie was looking at the man across the street as he detailed his whip.

"Nettie, did you hear me?" James asked breaking her out of the trance she was in.

"Huh, what did you say?" She looked at him.

"I said, can you let me hold something?"

She dug into her front pocket and handed him a twenty-dollar bill.

"Jay, you look like you already got ya head right," she said, noticing his sleepy eyes.

"I had a little something, but I'm still sick." He grabbed the money and shoved it into the pocket of his dingy jeans.

"All right. I'll see you later," Nettie said and stepped off the curb into the street and started across it. "I'm a republican" by Jay-Z and Nas was now blasting from the woofer speakers of the detailed car. The owner was digging around in the trunk of the vehicle and appeared to be looking for something.

"What's good, Meat?" Nettie asked as she stood behind him.

Meat stood upright and faced her. A huge smile appeared across his wide face.

"Hey, baby, what's good with you?" He bent down to give her a hug.

Meat stood six-five and weighed 300 pounds. He had a large head that sat on his broad shoulders. He acquired his name because of the excessive keloid skin that covered several spots on his head and face. The grotesque sight of the skin was nauseating at first sight. But those who knew him were used to it and simply looked past it.

Meat wasn't a bad-looking guy, but the large chunk of skin that covered the back of his neck and left cheek and the mass that hung from his left ear disguised his handsome features.

Meat had a crush on Nettie ever since they were teens attending the same public school. She was always nice to him and went to visit him when he came home from the hospital that horrible day. Even then, she still treated him fairly.

He was always a good kid and got good grades in school. He mostly stayed out of trouble and loved his mother to death. When he was just fifteen-years-old, his mother's boyfriend came home drunk one night. As usual, he started in on his mother, which normally led to him physically abusing her. Meat was tall for his age and always carried extra weight. That night, he'd heard enough of his mother's cries and pleas for help. He went into the kitchen and grabbed a knife from the drawer. He walked into his mother's bedroom and saw her boyfriend standing over her as she lay balled up in a fetal position. The boyfriend kicked and punched her at will. Meat slashed him across his back. Once he saw the blood soak the man's shirt, he became scared and dropped the knife.

Because of the man's inebriated state, he barely felt the pain. He whirled around, charged at Meat, grabbed him by the throat with both hands and began to choke him while yelling obscenities. Meat's mother jumped on the man's back in an attempt to save her son. Her actions distracted him and he let Meat go. He flung Meat's mother to the floor and kicked her in the head. He then turned to face Meat as he lay on the floor, trying to catch his breath.

"You wanna kill me, boy?" he yelled.

He picked up the knife from the floor and walked over to Meat. Fear consumed his body as the man leaned over and slashed Meat on the side of his face.

The pain raced down the left side of his face, causing him to scream out. Meat scurried to his feet. As he did this, the knife came down again, this time missing his face and slicing the bottom portion of his ear. Once on his feet, Meat turned to run out of the room. Before he could make it through the doorway, he felt air on the back of his neck, and then an unbearable pain. Liquid ran down the back of his neck and down the middle of his back. He placed his hand on the back of his neck as he stumbled forward. When he looked at his hand, it was covered with blood. The room began to spin and he fell to the floor, unconscious.

His wounds never healed properly, creating the keloid skin in each place he was slashed.

"Hey, daddy, how you doing?" Nettie hugged him back.

"Just cleaning the shoes on my whip." He stepped back

to look at his work.

"Yeah, I hear you. You got ya joint shining. I ain't even mad at you. You need to do something with my ride," Nettie said, looking across the street at her car parked in the driveway.

"That's you?"

"Yeah, that's me."

"That's a good look, Nettie."

"It's a little something, something. I need to upgrade, though. So I see you doing big things." She looked at his car. "So you still work at AT&T?"

"Yeah, I got promoted to VP of Sales three months ago."

"Damn, look at you, locking down the business world!" She smiled at him. "You always been smart. I knew you were gonna go places in your life."

"So where you been, Nettie? I haven't seen you in a minute."

"I been around, you know, doing this and that."

"I heard you was dancing up at the strip joint Bodilicious." He grabbed the towel from the trunk and began wiping down the already spotless vehicle.

"I used to dance there, but I gave up that life. The money just ain't coming in like it used to. But I'm on some other shit right now."

"Yeah, what's that?" he asked.

"Well, I can't really talk about it right now until I make sure that its official. But what I do need to know is: Can I count on you to have my back?" She looked up at him innocently. "I'm gonna need you."

"You know you my girl and I'll do anything for you. But

what I need to know is: Is it illegal?"

Nettie shifted her eyes to the ground and then back up at him.

"I'll tell you this. I'll make it worth your while if you have my back like I may need you to." She ran her hands over her jeans that hugged her body like a glove.

Meat followed her hands as they went down her thighs and back up again, brushing past her secret middle. He felt chills run down his spine.

"W-well Nettie, you know I-I got your back. Just tell me what it is that you n-need," he stuttered.

Nettie knew what she was doing. She knew the power of the pussy and she also knew that she wouldn't have to sex Meat to get what she wanted. She never did. It was no secret how he had always felt about her. She walked up to him and put her hand on his chest.

"I'll get at you when I'm ready. In the meantime, I'ma give you my number and let me get yours so I can call you."

CHAPTER 10

Meanwhile, in another town.

"**W**hat's up, papí!" Wild shouted as he walked into the bodega on Park Avenue in East Orange. The elderly Spanish man smiled.

"¿Que pasa, amigo?"

Wild walked over to the refrigerator, grabbed two, tall bottles of Lipton Green Tea and placed them on the counter.

"Papí, let me get a turkey and cheese sandwich and don't be stingy with the meat."

"OK, amigo." The elderly man walked around behind the counter, ready to prepare the sandwich. In the meantime, Wild threw a few Tasty Kakes and a couple bags of chips onto the counter.

Wild was six foot two with an athletic build. He had a bald head and thin sideburns connecting to a thin goatee. His name was self explanatory to those who knew him or knew of him. He didn't give a fuck about shit. Wild's motto was: "Nobody ever gave two shits about me, so why should I care about anyone else?" Wild was cut from a different cloth, as a kid, he went from foster home to foster home, from group home to boys' detention center and then to prison. He never knew his parents or anyone in his family. Word was that his mother was a prostitute and gave birth to him on the backseat of her john's car. The pimp wrapped Wild's newborn body in an old towel that he used to wipe his car down and then sat his crying body in a dumpster.

Although Wild dabbled with drug distribution and pimping, his current, acquired occupation of choice was robbing. He chose this occupation because he knew he was feared by most. The ones that didn't fear him also knew he was deranged and they usually stayed out of his way to avoid any confrontation. He robbed from the rich and stole from the poor, depending upon his mood. It didn't make him no difference who he took from. But, truth be told, Wild was getting tired of that life. There wasn't a challenge to it anymore. It was becoming boring to him and he wanted more power. So, his plan was to take out the top dog who ran Essex County and become king. His target was Leroy Jenkins.

The bell that was above the door chimed as it opened. In walked two young teens, talking loudly about the shooting that happened that morning in Newark. They looked up and saw Wild standing at the counter, looking their way. They knew exactly who he was.

They both gave him a head nod of acknowledgement and proceeded to get what they came in for.

"So them cats got they bodies twisted this morning, huh?" one of the young teens in a black, fitted Yankee cap asked.

"Word. I heard it was Day-Day and Unique," the other teen with a tan scully on his head said.

"Man, how you figure? Them cats always carry heat. They nice as hell with the armor. Ain't no way they let some niggas slump them like that," Yankee cap said as he stood back and looked at the selection of junk food, finally deciding on some *Dipsy Doodle* corn chips.

"Ay, I'm telling you, kid, them niggas got slumped. I heard some cats rolled up on the block spraying. They said Day-Day's head was lying next to his body when it was all over!" Tan scully recited the now already-exaggerated story.

"Get the fuck outta here!" the unbelieving teen in the Yankee cap shouted.

"Word, that's real talk."

The two boys tossed their junk food onto the counter, next to the food Wild had placed there just minutes earlier.

"A-Yo, papí! How much is this, man?" Yankee cap asked as he pulled a knot from his pocket and peeled off a twenty. "Yo, let me get a box of Switzer Sweet Peach flavored blunts, too. So what did Big Roy say about it?" he turned and asked Tan scully.

Wild stood there, towering over the boys, ice grilling them.

"Man, I don't know. When I went to pick up, nobody was saying a word. It looked like a morgue up in the joint. I just grabbed our shit and bounced up outta there. But, you could tell them niggas was on fire. I ain't even see Big Roy, but I could feel the heat in the place," Yankee cap said.

Just hearing Leroy's name gave Wild a hard-on. He wanted to get at Leroy in worst way.

"A-Yo, papí! Wassup man?" Yankee fitted asked with much attitude, speaking to the owner.

"One minute, amigo," the old man said as he continued

to prepare the sandwich. "Mama!" he called loudly.

An older Spanish woman came out from the back of the store. The elder man spoke to his wife in Spanish, clearly showing he didn't want the occupants in the store to know what he was saying. The older woman obliged and busied herself with ringing up the teens' purchase.

Wild stood back and observed the young boys and their expensive attire. The fact that the young teen pulled out a grip from his pocket confirmed that they were putting in work for Leroy. They also sported iced watches and chains. Wild shook his head. His motto was to never trick your money off on materialistic things, showing the world just how caked you were. People like himself observed shit like that, therefore making them obvious targets for the setup.

Wild knew some Spanish and understood what the old man had said to his wife. He now knew that the old man feared blacks and wanted to get them all out of the store. The man thought that they were trouble and didn't want them in the store for long, which pissed off Wild. As much money as the neighborhood spent in the store to help keep them in business and this was what they thought of black people?

The elderly lady rang up and bagged the teens' purchases. The teen boys grabbed their bags and stepped away from the counter, but not before they locked eyes with Wild one last time. They threw their heads up at him and proceeded out of the store.

Wild continued to stare at the door even after it had closed. He appeared to be deep in thought when the old man interrupted his contemplative moment.

"OK, amigo, your food ready." He smiled nervously and

nodded his head. He began to ring up and bag the items.

"Nine twenty-five, my friend," he said with his heavy accent.

"Nine twenty-five! For that little bit of shit!" Wild yelled.

"Please, amigo," he pleaded. "No problema, por favor."

"I'm not gonna give you any problems. I heard what you told your wife."

The old man's eyes became wide.

"Yeah, I heard what you said. We bring problems every time we come into the store, right?" Wild asked as the veins on the side of his head became visible. The back of his head began to ache and he felt the demon inside begin to rise. The old man gave a nervous smile.

"You 'peak a Spanish?"

"No, I don't 'peak a Spanish', muthafucka, but I understand some of it, papí. So, just for that, put the money in the bag with my shit!"

The old man began to sweat heavily.

"P-p-please, tiene familia. Me have family," the man stuttered.

"I don't give a fuck about yo' family!"

Wild pulled out a .357 and pointed it at the old man.

The store owner's wife threw her hands over her mouth and began to speak in Spanish.

"Oh, Dios mio! No nos lastime para satisfacer. Please, no hurt us," she cried.

Wild demanded the old man open the register and when he did, Wild reached over into the register, taking all the money inside and grabbed his bagged purchase off the counter. He tucked his gun back into its hiding spot and glided out of the store like he had made a legal purchase.

When Wild stepped outside he spotted the two young teens that had entered the store moments earlier, standing on the opposite corner. He made a mental note as he studied their faces again.

Two hours later, three teens were playing dice up against the side of a building. They each held cash in their hands as they boasted and argued over the last roll. The night's temperature had dropped even lower than what it had been earlier in the day. Just as one of the boys scooped up the dice from the ground, the sound of a gun cocking caused them all to look up. There stood Wild with a nine pointed at the trio.

"What's up, fellas?" Wild asked with a sinister grin on his face.

They all looked up and defeat fell across their faces. Two of the boys dropped their shoulders. They were just in the bodega with him earlier and couldn't believe Wild was now standing there, pointing a gun at their heads. The teen with the Yankee fitted cap stood up from the stooped position he was in just before Wild showed up.

"Make another move, baby boy, and you can call it a night," Wild warned.

The boy knew he was serious, so he froze in his spot.

"Run ya shit," he told the trio.

With about a grand, making his pockets fatter and two other guns in his possession, Wild stepped away from the corner and disappeared, leaving the young cats bent.

CHAPTER 11

Nate, Dice, and Click sat double-parked in a black S65 Benz, bopping their heads to *"There's Been A Murder"* by Jay-Z. Dice sat in the front passenger seat while Click took up the rear driver's side. Nate sat behind the wheel, looking agitated as he scratched his neatly trimmed, full beard.

"Where the hell this nigga at?" he questioned no one in particular.

Neither occupant said a word. Dice had retrieved a grape-flavored blunt from the pack, had carefully split it down the middle and held it out of the open passenger window, allowing the tobacco to fall to the ground.

Nate, now even more aggravated, laid on the horn. A couple that was walking on the opposite side of the street looked at him with questioning eyes. Nate caught their stares and hit the power windows to let the window down.

"What the fuck y'all looking at?" he yelled out the window.

"Yo, man, chill," Click said from the rear, already showing signs of being blunted.

"Why you tripping, yo?" Dice added.

"Y'all niggas shut the fuck up! If this nigga ain't out here in a minute, I'm out!" Nate exclaimed.

Just as the words passed his lips, the front door of the apartment building opened. Little Cash stepped out the door, sporting a pair of *Mecca* jeans with several patches on them. He walked gap-legged in an attempt to keep the pants from falling off his thin body. His white-on-white *Nikes* were covered by the sagging jeans, except for the toes. His fitted cap was pulled far down over his eyes; all that was visible was his nose and mouth. He held his head up high in an attempt to see where he was walking.

Nate started the ignition and put the car in gear. Little Cash hopped into the backseat with Click.

"What's up, fellas!" a cheerful Little Cash asked.

"What the fuck, man? What took you so long?" Nate asked as he drove down the street.

"I was getting dressed," Little Cash answered Nate in confusion.

"You act like a bitch, man! It don't take no nigga that long to throw some shit on, damn!" Nate continued to preach.

"Stop bitchin', man," Dice said as he filled the split blunt by crushing bud into it.

"Why you stuntin' on me, Nate?" Little Cash wanted to know.

"Man, fuck all that bullshit. Pass the blunt and let's get faded," Click spoke up.

The quad traveled down Clinton Avenue on their way to a meeting with Leroy. Since Ishmael's passing, they had teamed up with Leroy to keep their pockets fat. They had made several attempts to go out on their own as a team, but to no avail. Their attempts kept failing, partly because Nate, Dice and Click were security men. Their game was to inflict pain and stacking bodies was their forte. Little Cash was the drug handler; however, he didn't have much knowledge on how to get shit popping. So when all else failed, they got put on with Leroy who still controlled the county. Any other small-time hustler wasn't large enough to feed the kind of appetite they had for money.

Although they were now down with Leroy, they weren't satisfied. They ate with Leroy, but they weren't full. Leroy took them in like stray dogs. They were a part of Ishmael's crew and Nate had said on many occasions, "Leroy on some ol' feeling-sorry-for-a-nigga shit."

Nate felt that Leroy was keeping them close since Ishmael and Derrick's deaths. Maybe he thought they had something to do with Ishmael's death because they weren't around that night. But, truth be told, none of them knew a thing about what happened. All they knew was that Derrick was missing and Ishmael went on a rampage, looking for him.

That next day, when they found out about all the murders, they couldn't figure out what happened since they weren't in the loop. Little Cash took it the hardest, as he was the youngest of the quad and he admired Ishmael the most. The crew kept their ears to the streets afterward but kept coming up empty.

They pulled up in front of the pool hall and got out of the car. Walking inside, they headed for the office in the rear. Dak, the bodyguard, was standing in his usual spot near the office door. Nate threw his head up to acknowledge the big man. Dak got up, opened the door and they all walked in.

Leroy was sitting in his chair with his back to the door, on the phone, when they walked in. He never said a word or acknowledged their presence.

"So, Tony, tell me what I really need to know about this cocksucker, Detective Daniels."

Leroy was on the phone with the former mayor of Newark, Tony. After the murders took place that horrible night several months ago, the Mayor's right-hand man Bowens was killed and a lot of questions and accusation were thrown his way. The heat was too hot in the kitchen and the mayor broke camp, resigning before the new election. With the bad press he received and the indictment he possibly faced, his ultimate choice to resign was a wise one. Tony now resided in Florida and was trying to repair his life and political role in the community.

"Leroy, Rick Daniels is good police. He's respected in the community and I'd keep the eyes, in the back of my head, open if I were you," Tony said.

"But the son of a bitch don't have shit on me, Tony. I made sure everything was clean."

Dak cleared his throat in an attempt to warn Leroy of his presence. Leroy whirled his chair around, only to look into the faces of all four men.

"Hey, Tony, let me get back to you on that thing, cool?" Leroy disconnected the call. "Gentlemen, please make yourselves comfortable. It slipped my mind that we were meeting today."

Everyone took a seat, but no one said a word.

"So you wanted this meeting and now that you're here, what's on your minds?" Leroy asked.

They all looked at each other, trying to figure out who was going to be the spokesperson for the crew. Since Nate was much older than the rest of the quad, he took the bait and spoke first.

"Listen, Big Roy, we wanted to talk about our positions within this organization. Although we give you respect and ya props for letting us ride with you after Ishmael got killed . . ." Nate stopped speaking as if he was searching for the right words. They all knew that Leroy was a big man in town and his powers extended even farther than that. They also knew what kind of a man Leroy could be. So Nate knew he had to choose the right words to say in order to represent the quad.

"Big Roy, we were wondering when you were going to step up our game with some more profitable jobs. I mean, I know you already got your security team in place and they're strong. But we really ain't been puttin' in too much work."

Leroy kept his gaze on Nate and then he swept his eyes along the others. Everyone met his stare except Little Cash. He seemed uncomfortable and didn't want to make eye contact.

"So y'all niggas ain't eatin'?"

"Yeah, we eatin', Big Roy, but we ain't full like we used to be with Ish," Click added.

Leroy laughed. The quad looked at each other. Nate sat back in his chair with a disturbed look on his face. Patience was not one of his strong points, and as far as he could tell, Leroy was about to play them.

"Listen up, fellas, let me explain something to you. I did you muthafuckas a favor by putting you on. I did it out of respect for Ishmael. I knew Ishmael had a solid team and I didn't want to leave you out in the cold 'cause I know how that can be. But if you punks don't want to appreciate what I did for you, then move on, chumps. But if it was me, I would take this free money and live. Shit, you punks ain't really doing shit for me but taking up space and I'm still paying ya asses. That's free money." He held out his hand for Dak to give him some dap. They both laughed, but the quad sat there and didn't say a word.

"Here's the deal. Anybody who wants to ride can take this free ride, but anybody who feels froggish, then leap. Just know who you fuckin' with. On the other hand, if y'all little niggas wanna bounce and go out on ya own, by all means, do you. I ain't here to stop ya flow, 'cause whoever you cop from is copping weight from me, so in the end I'm still gonna make my paper. Feel me?"

The quad sat stone-faced and silent.

"Cool. Just let me know what you gonna do. Get at me in a week. If you that uncomfortable, then bounce, fellas. There won't be no hard feelings or repercussions. That's my word," he said, placing his fist over his heart.

CHAPTER 12

Wild sat in a Nissan Sentra that he'd rented with the money he lifted off the two dealers. It was a little after midnight and he was sitting a block away from the pool hall that Leroy owned.

He had been watching Leroy for a couple of weeks, learning his routine in and out. He knew how often Leroy switched vehicles and how often he left the pool hall. Sometimes he would stay at the pool hall until daybreak before Leroy left the premises and if Wild had access to a vehicle, he would follow Leroy home. Leroy's security was tight and they were very careful. Oftentimes they would take Wild on a wild goose chase when he followed them. But in the end, he outsmarted them and they led him right to Leroy's home in Livingston.

Wild had thought on one occasion that they knew he was following them. That was why he made sure that when he did have a vehicle, he drove a different vehicle the next time. This led to him renting cars instead of stealing them for the stakeout.

Wild was a master of most things and stealing cars was

a favorite of his when he was a young teen. He did five years in juvenile detention when he was eleven for attempted vehicular manslaughter.

It all happened one day while he sat on a crate on the side of the building of a storefront. A woman pulled up in a shiny, new, red Ford Mustang. She got out of her car, leaving it running just to run into the store. The adrenaline in Wild began to pump as he stood to his feet. He ran and jumped into the running vehicle and took off, not realizing there was a three-year-old girl asleep in her car seat. He sped down the street and skidded to a stop in front of two neighborhood kids with whom he attended school. One of the boys jumped in while the other was too scared to participate. They did doughnuts, leaving black circles on the pavement and screeched off down the street. When the little girl in the backseat began to cry, the boys panicked. Instead of pulling over and jumping out of the car, they pulled over, removed the entire car seat and sat the child on the sidewalk.

After twenty minutes more of joy riding, they wound up in a three-hour police chase through the city. Wild, being young and not that experienced in high-speed maneuvering, jumped the curb and mowed down several people at a bus stop, critically injuring an elderly woman. He crashed into and damaged countless cars. The speedometer sometimes reached up to ninety-five miles per hour on the city streets.

Finally, the police shot out two tires on the car, causing it to spin out of control, and flip seven times before landing on its roof. Wild's friend was thrown from the car and he ended up being paralyzed and wheelchair-bound.

Wild thought about robbing the pool hall on many

occasions after Leroy and his team left, but that wouldn't be satisfying enough for him. He wanted the big payoff— Leroy's status. The very next day, after he found out where Leroy lived, he thought of breaking into the house once Leroy left for the day. But after he carefully observed the grounds, he figured that wouldn't be a good idea. Leroy had security up the ass. Cameras were mounted at many different locations around the huge house and those were the ones he could see. Leroy had four Rottweiler's running on the grounds. He had security men posted up at different locations and walking the grounds.

Wild sat in thought as he watched the door to the pool hall as people went in and out. He was the mastermind, but this job wouldn't be easy for him to pull off by himself. He needed help and he knew it. However, he was a loner and didn't trust anyone. Wild knew he needed to either come up with a new plan or start recruiting. And in his case, with his rep, that meant putting fear into the hearts of those he would be recruiting. Either way, this move was gonna take longer than he expected.

After sitting there for another twenty minutes, Wild decided to call it a night. It didn't make sense to keep sitting there and following Leroy home when he wasn't gonna make a move and Wild wasn't big on wasting time.

Wild drove around the city aimlessly, not ready to return to the room he had rented in a run-down boarding house in East Orange. So, he decided stop over at the Bodilicious strip joint for a nightcap.

He found a parking spot in front of the club, which was unusual for a Saturday night. He killed the engine and hopped out of the car. A few people were posted up out front, politicking. He entered the club and took a seat at the far end of the bar. The club was semi-full, but the music was live. Strippers danced on the stage and some were working the crowd of men. Others were behind the bar, working their way around to each occupant.

Wild had been with many women in his lifetime, as he'd started sexing at a very young age, so to see a topless woman wearing a thong did nothing for him. He'd had the best of the best and the worst of the worst in women. At that point in his life, most women had no morals and they threw pussy at him even when he wasn't looking. Just like with everything else that he did, he needed a challenge, and there seemed to be no challenging pussy out there.

He was on his second shot of Grey Goose when in walked a beautiful work of art. She looked familiar to him, but he couldn't yet place where he'd seen her before. All Wild knew was that she was sexy as hell. She had a certain air about herself. She walked with confidence and arrogance, all at the same time. He noticed the way she carried herself, the way she held her head up high and her back straight. She was the perfect depiction of a woman.

Wild watched her. Everyone seemed to know her. Some people she stopped and talked with. Others she simply walked over as if they were rose petals strewn beneath her feet. She was being followed by three Hispanic beauties, all who seemed to walk in her glow. The quad headed over to the entrance of the dressing room where the strippers changed.

The thought came across his mind that maybe she was a stripper, but then he didn't want to believe that a woman showing such dominance would allow her morals to be so low as to strip.

Twenty minutes later, one of the Hispanic women entered the stage and began to do her routine. Wild kept his eye on the dressing room door, but he never saw the mystery woman come out. Fifteen minutes more and his patience had run out. He was ready to give up on seeing her again, so he stood to leave.

None of the dancers had even attempted to approach him in the time he sat at the bar. It wasn't because no one liked him or even knew who he was. Wild was an attractive man and any woman would love to get next to him, but it was the unapproachable look he kept plastered on his face that kept everyone that didn't know him at bay.

Giving up on seeing her again tonight, Wild walked toward the door. He turned and looked one last time before exiting the club.

CHAPTER 13

"Yo, man, get yo' feet off my fuckin' table! I don't come to yo' crib, putting my feet on yo' shit," Nate said to Click.

"Shut the fuck up, man. You been bitchin' all day," a very blunted Click said.

He was sitting on the sofa in Nate's living room in the deepest of leans, as his high was taking him to a new level. The goods they had been smoking all day seemed to have lasted an eternity, as the last blunt they smoked was two hours ago.

"Yo, dog, fire up," Click drawled, just above a whisper.

"Man, chill. We need to be tryna figure out what fuck we gonna do. So, y'all niggas still wanna roll with Big Roy and his bullshit or what?" Dice asked from the recliner he was sitting in.

Little Cash snored at the other end of the sofa that Click sat on.

Nate was sitting in the other recliner. He picked up the remote off the arm of the chair and threw it at Little Cash in an attempt to wake him. The remote hit the young boy in the chest, which caused him to jump straight up off the sofa. The dumb look on his face caused everyone else in the room to burst out in laughter.

Little Cash plopped back down onto the sofa, irritated. "Man, y'all niggas play too much!"

The trio continued to laugh, but Little Cash didn't see the humor.

"Aight, y'all chill. No, but on some real shit, what y'all wanna do? Because frankly, I ain't tryna be Big Roy's bitch for long. That ain't even my MO," Nate said seriously.

"Word," Click chimed in.

"I say we say fuck it and do what we do on our own," Dice added.

"Yeah, but we already tried that shit and you heard what Big Roy said. It don't matter who we cop from. That nigga gonna still get his paper. Y'all tryna do it like that?" Nate looked into each of their faces.

"So whatchu saying, Nate?" Dice asked.

Nate sat there a moment longer, thinking before he spoke.

"I think old man Leroy had a good run. Ishmael ain't here to step up in his spot, so . . ." Nate stopped talking to make sure he had everyone's attention.

Click sat upright on the sofa with a look of intensity. Dice raised the chair to its upright position and sat forward with his elbows resting on his knees. But Little Cash still sat relaxed in the corner of the sofa and hadn't caught on to what Nate was saying.

Nate, Dice, and Click were beasts and craved blood at all times, so although doing Leroy would be different from what they were used to, the hunger was still lurking and running through their veins.

"So whatchu saying?" Little Cash asked, clueless.

Everyone turned their attentions to Little Cash, mean mugging him.

"What?" he questioned.

Click leaned over and punched him in the chest.

"Come on, chill." Little Cash put his hand up to his chest where the stinging had started.

"So, Nate man, do you think we can take Big Roy?"

"How you sound? Just look at it like this. We couldn't be no closer than we already are. We already down with him, so all we gotta do is come up with a plan. We need a plan that's gonna eliminate him and his muscle," Nate said with confidence.

"Yo, man, do you hear how you sound? On everything I love, I got yo' back no matter what and you know that. But Big Roy is a hard nigga to get next to. You really think that shit is gonna stop with Big Roy if we body his ass? No, it's a whole lotta other muthafuckas on his team that's just waiting for that day, 'specially Dak."

"Fuck Dak!" Dice said.

"Word," Nate co-signed as he looked at Click.

"A'ight, man, so what's the plan?" Click sat back, defeated.

"First we gonna go back to Big Roy and tell him we gonna ride with him. But that's just our front, you feel me?"

Everyone nodded in agreement. Little Cash sat there daydreaming. He was thinking about Ishmael, which he often did. He couldn't understand how his idol allowed someone to catch him slippin' and take his life. He didn't believe it then and still couldn't believe it now. Not the Ishmael that he knew. He had a special relationship with Ishmael that most of the other guys didn't know about. There would be times when Ishmael would come around to the blocks Little Cash was working and Cash would hop in the truck with him. Ishmael would talk to him for an hour or two about life and the business. Little Cash believed Ishmael told him things that he didn't share with anyone else. He remembered on one occasion that Ishmael was thinking about getting out of the game and making a life with Desiree.

Little Cash had thought about doing the same since Ishmael's death. He was still young and the life he was leading was getting him nowhere fast. He hated hanging around with Nate and the rest, of the quad because they treated him unfairly. They always shorted him on the money when Leroy hit them off. Cash had a sick mother, two little brothers and a sister to take care of. Ishmael gave him guidance and he paid him well. Now Ishmael was dead and there was no one to turn to. It just didn't sit right with him and seemed strange on how it all went down. Something wasn't right and often Little Cash attempted to get some information on the murders, unbeknownst to the others.

"Cash, man!" Nate called out to him, breaking him out of his deep thoughts.

Little Cash looked bewildered.

"What's up, Nate?" Little Cash was tired of Nate bossing him around.

"You ain't heard shit I said, did you? Yo, you better get yo' head out yo' ass."

Little Cash just looked at Nate nonchalantly as he

continued to tell the rest of the crew the plan.

Two hours later Little Cash walked out of Nate's place and descended down the front steps. It was two a.m. and he began the long walk back to his neighborhood. He could've easily asked for a ride or caught a cab, but he felt he needed the walk to clear his head. He was the only one out of the crew who didn't have a car.

After walking in the frigid cold for about twenty minutes he walked past the Bodilicious strip club as occupants were leaving the club for the night. The hustlers were posted up next to their whips as the hood rats and groupies hung around, trying to get noticed for the all-American, come-up dream date with one of them. Some of the dancers exited the club with their catch of the night, heading home for a night of one-night-stand, sexing.

Little Cash gave dap to some of the fellas that he knew and kept it moving.

"Cash!" Someone called his name.

He turned back toward the club to see Nettie approaching him. He stopped and waited until she caught up to him.

"What's good, Cash?" she asked, looking as lovely as ever.

"It's all good, Nett." He smiled, admiring how beautiful she was. "Whatchu doing here? I heard you don't dance anymore."

"I don't, but my peeps still dance, so I usually come down to give them support."

"Word."

"So where you been, man? I haven't seen you in a while," she said.

"I been chillin'. You know how that is."

"Sorry about what happened to ya boy, Ish," she said, feeling the need to tell him while trying to look sincere. Deep in her heart, Nettie could've careless about his death. In her mind that was one less asshole roaming the streets. Although she didn't have anything to do with his death, she wished she had and that could be one reason why he kept appearing her dreams.

"Please, Nett. You ain't even like Ish," Little Cash said, not believing that she actually cared.

"I mean, we had our beefs, but I ain't wish for the nigga to die. He was with my girl Zola first, way before Desiree came into the picture and took him from her. Which was cool with me but now that she's gone, that shit still hurts. You feel me?" Nettie now looked hurt as she thought about her ex-lover, Zola.

"Yeah, I feel you." Little Cash said knowing the history of Zola, whom he never liked anyway.

They both stood there for an awkward moment before Nettie spoke again.

"So, who you running with now?"

"Big Roy," he said.

"Oh, you with Big Roy now?" Nettie asked with a raised brow.

"Yeah."

"You don't look too happy about that. Getting down with Big Roy was a major move on your part."

"It ain't all that, Nett."

The wheels in Nettie's brain began to spin. She reached into her purse, pulled out a pen and a piece of paper and began to write.

"I always liked you, Cash. You always been a cutie to me. Here, take my number and hit me up when you get some free time. I got something in the works and I can always use a good cat like yourself on my team. There's major paper to be made and I'm about to get it poppin'," she said, handing him the paper.

Little Cash took the paper and smiled at Nettie. He was thinking about more than just getting paper with Nettie as he looked her up and down, undressing her with his eyes.

"Hit me, Cash, all right?" she asked, walking away.

Little Cash stood there a few more moments and watched the fatty that was mounted on Nettie's backside sway from side to side before continuing his journey home.

CHAPTER 14

Another day

As Nettie drove she thought about the nightmare she just had the night before. This time she was tied to a chair and Derrick used a sharp hunter's knife to carve the nipples off her breasts. She rubbed her hand along her titties almost feeling the pain it caused in her dream. It was true she killed Derrick by slicing off his dick and subsequently cutting his throat, even though she was starting to like him in the small amount of time they shared together. But business was business, nothing personal. There was money to be made and *nothing* stands in the way of Nettie making her paper.

Nettie pulled up to the corner and stopped. The passenger door opened and Little Cash hopped in.

"What's up, Nett?" He closed the door after getting in.

"What's up, Cash?"

She pulled off from the corner.

"A'ight, so what's up? You said there was major paper to be made," Little Cash said, getting straight to the point.

"Well there is, but I need to know that I can trust you,

Cash." She looked over at him.

"Come on, Nett, I'm ya man right now. I'm lookin' for a new home anyway."

"So what about Nate and 'em?"

"What about 'em? Them niggas on some other shit. . . ." Little Cash trailed off.

"What?"

"Nothing, man. Don't worry about it."

"No, for real, Cash. What's up? What they up to?"

"I can't really talk about it, Nett."

"So what, you don't trust me?" She egged him on.

"It ain't that. I mean, them niggas would split my skull if I told you." He looked at her seriously.

Nettie knew the deal with Nate, Dice, and Click. She knew they were hungry soldiers and could be very useful as security for her. In fact, she felt she could use them for what she was about to do. All they wanted was fat pockets and she knew that once she came up, they would be quick to get down with her. But that would have to come later.

"A'ight, Cash, I feel you, babe. I gotta swing by my mom's crib right quick, a'ight?"

"I'm straight, Nett. Do you," he said, reclining the seat back and pulling the brim of his fitted down further over his eyes.

Twenty minutes later they pulled into the driveway of Nettie's mother's house.

"Come on," Nettie said as she opened the car door and got out.

Little Cash hopped out of the car and stretched. He walked around the back of the car and hopped up the steps two at a time. Nettie was already partially in the house and holding the door open for him. Little Cash stepped into the foyer and removed his baseball cap. He brushed his hand over his waves in an attempt to make sure they were lying down, then he followed Nettie down the hall and into the living room where her mother's wheelchair sat in front of the TV.

"Hey, Ma." Nettie kissed her mother on the cheek.

"Hey . . ." Carolyn stopped and stared at Little Cash.

"How you doing, ma'am?" he asked shyly.

"Jeanette, who this little nigga you bringing up in my house? How do you know if I was dressed or not?" Her mother grilled her.

"Oh, come on, Ma, he good peoples. He a friend of mine. Come on and sit down, Cash," she said to him.

Nettie's mother continued to stare at him as she looked at his sagging pants when he walked past her and sat on the sofa.

The baby boy began to stir in the playpen where he was sleeping. He lifted his head and began to whine. Nettie walked over, picked up the baby and brought him over to the sofa, sitting him on her lap.

"What's up, little man?" She grabbed his little hand.

The baby rubbed his eyes and continued to whine.

"Here, Cash. Hold him while I go get a diaper for him." She placed the baby in his arms.

The baby looked up at Little Cash, bewildered. He continued to stare at him because he didn't know him. Little Cash looked into the baby's eyes and realized they were green.

"Hey, little man." He rubbed the baby's cheek as he spoke to him.

"His name is Nyeem." Nettie's mother spoke up as she continued to stare at Little Cash. "Are you the father of that there baby?"

"No, ma'am." Little Cash was quick to answer.

Just then Janet walked into the living room. Little Cash looked up to see her and was astonished. He couldn't break the stare he was giving her.

Janet walked over to the entertainment center and removed a piece of mail she had been looking for. She turned and looked at Little Cash.

"What are you looking at?" she asked him with her hand now on her hip.

"I-I-um, how you doing?" he asked.

"Who are you? Who is this, Mommy?" She looked to her mother for answers.

"I don't know. Some stray off the street Jeanette brought up in here," Carolyn said in disgust with no consideration for Little Cash's feelings.

"Is that your baby?" Janet asked him.

"Naw," Little Cash said, shaking his head.

Nettie walked back into the living room with the Pamper in her hand.

"I know y'all ain't messing with him." Nettie looked from her sister to her mother.

"Ain't nobody doing nothing. He sitting here, stuck on stupid, staring at me like he ain't got no sense," Janet said and walked out of the room. "And stop bringing niggas up in here. You don't live here!" she said over her shoulder as she left the living room.

"Nettie, what is it that you want?" Carolyn asked.

"What are you talking about, Ma?" she asked as she took the baby from Little Cash.

"Come on, now, I ain't no fool. You done been here twice in two weeks. That's the most I've seen you in years. I hope you coming to get this baby soon."

"Come on, Ma, why I gotta be wanting something? I just thought I'd start visiting more often because you complain so much that I ain't here."

"Yeah, if you say so, Jeanette. You must think I'm some kinda fool." She turned her attention back toward the television.

"Well, to be honest with you, I do need a favor," she said as she began to change the baby's Pamper. He still stared at Little Cash with those beautiful green eyes.

"I knew it was something. So, come on out with the bullshit," Carolyn said.

"No bullshit, Ma. Can you give me Uncle Calvin's number?"

Uncle Calvin was Carolyn's younger brother. He was a Podiatrist and lived in Pennsylvania.

"Whatchu want with Calvin's number, Jeanette?"

"I need to talk to him about something."

"About what, Jeanette?" she asked a little too loudly, startling the baby.

"Ma, I haven't talked to my uncle in a minute and I just want to call him and say hi."

"Yeah, right," Carolyn said, unconvinced.

Nettie sucked her teeth and got up from the sofa, leaving

the baby lying there, looking up at Little Cash.

Ten minutes later they were getting into her car. Nettie backed out of the driveway and began to drive back over to the other side of town. She stopped at the red light and retrieved her cell phone from her purse. She pulled a piece of paper out and began to dial the numbers.

"Hey, Uncle Calvin, this is your niece, Jeanette. I was calling to say hi, so give me a call when you get this message. My number is . . ." After changing the baby's pamper and realizing Carolyn wasn't going to give her the number she went into her mother's purse and retrieved the number from her phone book.

She left her cell phone number and closed her phone. They continued to drive in silence until Little Cash spoke up.

"Yo, Nett, I didn't know you had a sister."

"There's a lot you don't know about me, Cash," she said, concentrating on the road.

"So whose baby is that?" He looked at her.

"Why?" She looked at him curiously.

"Because your mother and your sister asked me if I was the father."

"Don't pay them no attention. They be tripping at times." She waved her hand in dismissal.

Little Cash sat heavy in thought while he watched the scenery pass by.

CHAPTER 15

The next night

Maria walked into the living room carrying a tray that held six glasses half filled with wine. Seated in the living room were four women—two Hispanic, one Chinese, and one black. They all looked like supermodels, sporting makeup and superb attire.

The two Hispanic women, Marisa and Jasmine, were sisters and Maria's first cousins. The Chinese woman's name was Yuming, and the black woman's name was Shawnee. They were all dancers from the Bodilicious strip club. These women had been dancing at the club for more than five years. They all were cool with each other and got along well. They were about their business and worked at the club strictly for cash. Each woman was a hustler in her own right and loved to get money by any means necessary. They respected each other's hustle, no matter what it was.

So when Maria pulled them each aside and told them that Nettie wanted them to be involved in a deal that was going to put them on the map, they jumped at the opportunity. Dollar signs danced in all of their eyes at the mention of getting hit off big with major dough.

Maria invited them all over to her apartment for the first meeting of Nettie's great plan. Nettie and Maria had agreed that they would start off with the women first and feel them out before they set out to recruit the men for their muscle. Nettie thought that women were better thinkers and had more patience to get the ball rolling.

She had tried to reach her uncle again and when she finally did, she could tell just by the way he spoke to her that her mother had gotten to him first. He had told her that he'd received her voicemail message but her phone number was cut off at the end of the message. So, when he called her mother to get her number, Carolyn told him that whatever Nettie was asking, not to trust her. This pissed Nettie off so she tried to convince her uncle that she was living right and just needed to borrow a few dollars to get on her feet. Uncle Calvin was not biting the line Nettie threw to him. She had to rethink her plan of how she was going to find the money to get product to start her new found business of drug distribution.

Her plan to take Leroy Jenkins out was going to take careful, time-consuming planning. So, in the meantime and in between time, she needed to at least set things up to get some loot rolling in. After she and Maria did some brainstorming, they came up with a brilliant plan in which Little Cash would play a big part. Nettie and Little Cash hung out all day the day before and she had been drilling him with questions about Leroy's distribution process. She manipulated him into thinking that Leroy was straight playing him and the others but she just wanted to put him on for right now. She told him not to say anything to the others until they were set. By then, Nate and the rest of the crew would see how large Little Cash was living and would want to get down with them.

This made Little Cash think: He was the youngest of the crew and they always ragged on him and treated him like he knew nothing. They made him feel like they just allowed him to hang around them, when in reality he was the one who actually had the sit-down with Leroy so that they all could be brought into the organization. Little Cash never got the credit because Nate took over like it was his idea. Little Cash wanted to do something to show the quad that he could stand on his own even though he was nineteen-years-old and he still lived at home with his mother.

Nettie walked out of the bedroom and into the living room to greet the ladies. Maria handed her a glass of wine and took her seat on the loveseat next to Yuming. Nettie took a deep drink of her wine. She placed the glass on the entertainment center and turned around to face the women, who were waiting for her to speak.

"Ladies, thanks for coming out. I know some of you have to work tonight, so I won't take up much of your time. Maria has explained to you about my plan on how we can all stack major loot. That part is true. However, she didn't go into details on what it is that I need from all of you." She looked into each of their faces, studying them and then continued. "This plan is very dangerous and some of us may check out before we make it out."

"'Scuse me, Nettie?" Jasmine interrupted.

Nettie looked at her but didn't answer.

"What you mean, check out?" Jasmine asked.

"Die," Nettie said, looking deep into Jasmine's eyes.

Jasmine held her stare and didn't blink. Nettie continued with her speech.

"I'm going to ask that there are no more interruptions until I am completely done, cool?"

Everyone nodded their heads in agreement while Jasmine's sister Marisa rolled her eyes at Jasmine. Jasmine stuck up her middle finger at her sister and turned her attention back to Nettie.

"As I stated, some of us may not make it out alive. It is very dangerous and I need to know that I can trust each and every one of y'all." She pointed at each of them. "I need to know that I wasn't wrong for picking y'all to get down with me and Maria. This shit here is serious. It's confidential and I don't need nobody fucking up. If you don't think you can handle that type of pressure, you are free to bounce. But, just know, if you bounce and it gets back to me that you were snitching or running ya mouth, know that I will kill you myself. So the best thing for y'all to do is roll with it and handle ya business coming out on top. Do y'all feel me?"

No one said a word. Nettie definitely had their undivided attention, if she didn't before. Each woman sitting in that room knew that Nettie was true to her word and would, without a doubt, probably kill any one of them, at will. The rumor about Nettie and her blade was serious. Although none of them had ever seen her in action, they had all seen the blade she carried in her mouth.

"So, I say that to ask: Who wants to step off, and who wants to be down?"

Everyone looked around at each other to see who was going to raise up out of their seats first, or who was going to stay. No one stood to leave, but Nettie didn't say a word. She continued to stand there, staring at each of them, trying to read their faces. She wanted to look deep into their eyes, through to their souls, to see who was weak. After a few minutes of this, she was satisfied that she had indeed picked the right crew to help her with her plan.

She sat down in a chair that Maria had brought in from the kitchen table and began to explain the oath to the women.

"The first rule of this oath is to keep ya mouth shut. You say nothing to no one, except to another member only. If you get caught, you say nothing. You are all in this shit for life. This game don't have a revolving door because once you're in and you try to get out, you die. Anyone who wants to walk away can't be trusted outside of the circle. You will all keep your jobs at the club. You have to have a place of employment for cover-up purposes. You need to keep working in the club because a lot of information flows through the joint that can be very useful to us in the long run."

Nettie got up and went into the kitchen. She came back out with the bottle of wine and poured herself another glass. She did this on purpose, to let what she had just said soak into the women's heads. Nettie sat back down and looked up at them.

"Before I go to the next rule of oath, does anyone want

to walk out now?"

Everyone shook their head. Yuming had moved to the edge of the couch, showing interest in what Nettie was talking about. Nettie smiled to herself. She knew Yuming would be down for the crown. She was just that type of woman, eager to kick some ass at all times. Yuming had a black belt in Karate and her hands were registered as lethal weapons. She was the only Asian chick that was accepted in the hood.

"Cool. The next rule is money over niggas. Ain't no dick worth losing paper over. Dick come a dime a dozen and I am not saying that just because I like to eat pussy, because I love me some dick too."

Shawnee's face showed disgust.

"You got a problem with that, Shawnee?" Nettie noticed her facial expression.

"Listen, bitch, you do what you do. I ain't got shit to do with that. I just don't need to see it or hear about it. Frankly, I prefer a good stiff one and that's real talk, feel me?" Shawnee's eyes threw prisms at Nettie.

"I ain't got a problem with you loving dick, but like I said, money over dick any day, all day. You feel *me*?" Nettie grilled her right back.

"Cool with me," Shawnee said, taking a sip of her wine.

"So long as we understand each other, and let me get you bitches straight right now. It ain't no secret that I eat pussy. Y'all already know that shit and I ain't tryna eat none of y'all's funky twats, so let's kill that thought right now. This here is business, and I mean business. I picked y'all because y'all ain't the catty type of chicks. I need down bitches on my team, so I don't want no drama and cat fighting on my team, feel what I'm saying?"

"No doubt," Shawnee answered first. The rest chimed in after her.

"A'ight, like I said, money over niggas. Next rule, and a very important rule. Don't be out here trickin' ya money off, stuntin' and shit. We don't need to bring attention to ourselves. When you think muthafuckas ain't watching, that's when they're watching you the most. Remember y'all, are some stripper bitches and yes, the money is good, but it ain't that good to be walking 'round here in fur coats and shit. So keep a low profile and spend ya money in small quantities.

"So, we gonna be banking dineros like that, mamí?" Marisa asked.

"I told y'all, this ain't no joke. I'm talking this thing right here is gonna put us on the map!"

"That's what I'm talkin' 'bout, Nettie." Yuming reached over and gave Nettie some dap.

Nettie smiled and gave Yuming dap back. She thought Yuming was the coolest chick she'd ever met.

"A'ight, ladies, calm down," Nettie said in order to quiet the buzzing woman.

Everyone became quiet and gave Nettie their undivided attention again.

"And last but not least is trust. We gotta trust each other. If we don't have trust, we don't have shit. We ride together and we die together. Simple as that. If any of y'all got differences in this room, now is the time to get that shit out in the open and squashed. I don't want nobody on my team and they feelin' some kind of way about another member. I ain't having

that shit and you don't want to fuck with me. I will cancel
any of y'all asses if I find out that there is some beef between
members." With that said and done, Nettie stood to her feet
and downed her second glass of wine.

"Marinate on that for a minute. Talk amongst ya 'selves
and I'll be back. Maria, come on." She walked toward the
bedroom with Maria in tow. Once inside, Maria closed the
door behind her.

"¿Que pasa, mamí?" she asked, sitting down next to
Nettie on the bed.

"What do you think? Do you think they'll have our
backs?" Nettie asked.

"I think so, mamí."

"Who do you think is weak out there?"

Maria placed a manicured nail in her mouth, like she was
deep in thought.

"I can speak for my cousins, Netta. They some scandalous
bitches and we can trust them because we don't play when
it comes to having the family's back. I also know for a fact
Shawnee is a crazy bitch and she loves money, so she should
be good. And you know Yuming is definitely the right person,
if no one else is."

Nettie sat there, staring at the floor.

"Yeah, Yuming is perfect. I wish I had three more like her.
But we have to be absolutely sure, Maria."

"I feel good about who we picked, Netta. Don't worry."
Maria patted Nettie on the knee.

"Okay, let's do this thing, then."

They walked back into the living room and Nettie took
her seat and began to explain the plan to the women.

CHAPTER 16

It was one thirty a.m. and the main stash house had just received the flock of birds. Five head males sat around a large table and began to break the product down for street distribution. Two of them wore surgical masks because of the allergies both were born with. Inhalation of the chemicals threatened their ability to breathe so they both carried inhalers for their asthma.

Each occupant at the table ranged in age from seventeen to twenty-one. One man stood leaning against the wall near the front door and one stood at the rear door. They each carried artillery weapons and wore body armor underneath their clothing.

This was one of Leroy's main stash houses. He had several more stash houses located in various spots throughout Essex County, with Newark, Irvington and East Orange being his biggest profit cities.

The room was quiet, all except for the noise that was made by the workers processing the product. An occasional cough could be heard from the room. They were in a three-bedroom townhouse located in the center of the development. The development, located in a peaceful neighborhood, was newly built and housed middle-class families.

Leroy owned several other townhouses in the development, which were located on each outer corner. This was an extra security precaution for the stash house. At least two security men occupied the houses at all times so that all incoming and outgoing activity could be constantly monitored.

As the men worked diligently, the dealer in charge, named Stacks, stood and took a deep stretch.

"Looks like this gon' be a long night, fellas," he announced and took his seat again.

"Not if you put in the work and don't start bumpin' your gums like you always do," his right-hand man Dave said without stopping what he was doing.

Stacks was a short, stocky dude. He was clean-shaven and wore a mini afro with long, thin sideburns. Stacks' status ranked over the others at the table. They answered to him and he was the one to deal with Leroy's head man directly. He acquired his name by making large amounts of money for Leroy.

"Nigga, I put in more work on and off the streets than you could ever do," Stacks bragged.

"Yeah, you put in more work than me at running ya yap," Dave said.

The others at the table began to laugh. It was true that Stacks was a lotta mouth. He was a clown who loved attention so he talked loud and bragged even more. Leroy liked him most because he could back up every word that came out of his mouth. He was fearless and heartless. That's what landed him his position in the organization.

"Man, fuck you," Stacks spat as he reached behind his ear and removed the pre-rolled blunt that was resting there.

"I know you ain't about to light that shit up in here. You know damn well there ain't no smoking in the joint," one of the security men bellowed as it caught the attention of the others.

"Whatever. Y'all niggas be on some ol' bullshit. How Big Roy gonna even know I was blazin'? What, y'all gonna snitch on me?"

No one moved or said a word. The security men glared him with piercing eyes. Stacks got the picture.

"Y'all some pussies," he blurted out and stood, walking over to the backdoor. "I'm going out back to smoke this. Anybody wanna hit it?" He looked back at everyone in the room. No one moved. In fact, they all just kept working. Stacks shrugged his shoulders and stepped out of the back door into the cold night air. He sat down on one of the folding chairs on the back patio deck and lit the blunt. He inhaled deeply and held up his head, looking into the starlit sky while he blew the smoke from his lungs.

Meanwhile, a black Nissan Altima with midnight-tinted windows pulled into the townhouse development. It traveled past the first security spot and followed the winding road. Not even twenty seconds had passed when a navy blue Nissan Altima pulled into the development, following the same path as the black Altima.

The security guard at the first security townhouse sat up

in his chair and stared at the security monitor. He pushed a few buttons to allow the other security cameras to pick up both vehicles as they traveled down the road inside the development.

"Yo, you know them cars?" guard number one asked his partner, who had been nodding off in his comfortable, recliner-type rocking chair.

"Where?" he asked, wiping the saliva that was leaking from the corners of his mouth.

"Right there. The two Altimas." Guard number one pointed to the third camera.

"Naw, I ain't never seen them whips before, but them rims on the black joint are fire, though." Guard number two continued to watch the cars.

Guard number one looked over at guard number two like he stole something.

"You's a stupid muthafucka. I ain't talking 'bout the shoes on the whips. Man, just go back to sleep!" He pulled his Nextel walkie-talkie from his hip and hit the button for the chirp.

There were only three monitors in the room and each could only show a certain part of the development. Once the cars were out of range of those three cameras, the monitors were of no use to them.

"What's up?" A voice answered the chirp.

"Yo, check ya eyes for two Nissan Altimas, one black and one blue," guard one said into the handset. "You see 'em?"

"Yeah, I got a visual. What's up?"

"Do you recognize those whips?" guard one asked.

"Naw, I don't, but I got 'em in my view so I'll watch 'em

from here," guard number three said.

Guard number three pulled his chair closer to the table where his three security monitors sat. He began pushing buttons and adjusting the knobs to get a better visual on both cars.

"What's up?" his partner asked, coming back into the room from using the bathroom.

"We got two unknown vehicles that might be suspicious."

"Did you check the plates?" guard number four asked.

"I'm zooming in on them now." He continued to work the knobs on the equipment.

Each residence's vehicles were registered with the office. License plates and personal information for each tenant was on file. Any visitors or friends' vehicles were registered with the office. There was only one way in and one way out of the development by car. There were two security booths located at the entrance and the exit of the development. Two unarmed security guards occupied the booths and most of the lazy workers were either asleep or out walking the grounds at the wee hours of the night. Leroy and the owner of the development were business partners, so Leroy had access to the tenants' personal records.

"Nope, they're not on the list," guard number four said.

"We better call for someone to go check them out."

"Wait, they pulling into unit C. Let's see what's up."

Guard number three opened the books and began to run his finger down the list.

"Nobody lives in unit C," he said.

"Well, it looks like two women are getting out of the cars, and damn!" guard number four said.

"Maybe they new here. I think I need to go over and pay them a visit, you know, welcome them to the neighborhood," guard number three said, standing after catching a glimpse of the women.

"Oh, hell naw! You think you slick, nigga. I'm going with you. It's two of them," guard number four protested.

Both security guards were built like prison inmates. Their bodies were physically fit and they had muscle on top of muscle. They weren't the best looking fish in the pond but women fell for them because of their Mr. Universe-like physiques. And, as usual, they were thinking with their dicks.

They walked out of the townhouse without their weapons and descended the steps, heading toward unit C, which was located around the bend of the road about five townhouses away.

Over at unit C, the two females each stood at the rear of their vehicles. The first female put her hands up to her ear and then signaled the second female with a thumb's up. They each stuck the key of their respective vehicles into the trunks' locks and opened the trunks simultaneously. Two females wearing masks, all black, leather cat suits and cropped, black, leather jackets jumped out the trunks of each car. The four females carried black duffel bags that draped across their shoulders. These four women ran up the grassy hill and disappeared into the bushes, leaving the two female drivers behind.

Just as the two female drivers closed the trunks and stepped onto the sidewalk, the two security guards stepped around the corner.

"Ladies, my name is Leon. Is there anything that I can help you with?"

"And I'm Brian," the other guard chimed in before Leon could finish his introduction.

Both woman stared at the two bulky men and then looked at each other, laughing. The first female used her finger to seductively gesture to Leon for him to come closer. He obliged with a wide grin on his face as his eyes swept her body. She was wearing a pair of winter white, stiletto, thigh high boots with a winter white, leather, coochie skirt and a short winter white fur coat. The second woman sported tight-fitting Brat jeans, knee high, black, leather stiletto boots and a short, black, leather riding jacket. Despite the cold, they wore the zipper down on the jacket, purposely exposing mounds of cleavage.

As soon as Leon was in arms' reach, Nettie, the woman dressed in winter white, spit out the blade she was concealing in her mouth and struck Leon across his neck within seconds. It all happened so fast that Brian was still looking with unbelieving eyes before it registered for him to go into defense mode, but his reaction was too slow. Two slugs hit the back of his head, sending pieces of skull and brain matter flying. Blood and flesh splattered on Nettie's and Maria's faces and clothing.

CHAPTER 17

Stacks sat on the patio, still smoking the blunt, when he heard a noise come from the darkness of the yard. He looked out into the yard trying to see what could have made the sound. When he didn't hear anything else, he kept toking on the blunt. Once he was done, he tossed the roach to the deck's floor and stomped out the fire. Stacks stood to his feet, stretched and staggered over to the back door. Just as he was about to place his hand on the doorknob he was put into a choke hold and a gloved hand pressed firmly to his mouth. He struggled to break loose and was almost successful until a gun was placed firmly against his temple. Stacks stopped moving and relaxed his broad shoulders.

His weapon was then removed from the small of his back. The masked assailant moved Stacks to the side of the door and out of sight. The female holding the gun moved with them, keeping the gun in place. Another masked female tapped on the backdoor with nun chucks she retrieved from the duffel bag she was carrying. When the door opened and the guard poked his head out, she hit him in the face with the nun chucks, cracking the bridge of his nose. The pain caused the guard to drop his semi-automatic weapon to the deck floor. She then bent to pick up the weapon and delivered a karate sweeping motion with her leg, taking the security guard's legs out from under him. The big man hit the floor fast and hard, hitting his head and knocking himself unconscious. The sound alerted everyone in the townhouse to an intrusion. The second guard inside wasted no time letting off repeated rounds. Bullets ripped through the backdoor, but the masked woman with the nun chucks had crawled out of range and stood on the other side of the door. She signaled for the fourth masked woman who was standing down below on the ground, to go around front. The fourth masked woman ran around to the front door, picked the lock and let herself inside while the guard continued to reload and buck shots at the backdoor.

The dealers once sitting at the table hit the floor and ran for cover. Those carrying guns were now holding them, ready to fire and trying to figure out what was happening. All they knew was that the guard was bucking wildly at the backdoor.

In the meantime, the masked woman had entered the house and now had the guard in sight. She took aim and let off two shots—one bullet hitting the guard in the back of the neck and the other in the back of his head. The guards had on bulletproof vests but they did nothing to protect their heads. The guard's body dropped to the floor with a loud thud.

No one knew what had happened, but they all began to fire into the room from which they believed the shots had come. As they were doing this the other three masked women stepped into the house through the backdoor holding Stacks out in front, shielding them. The gun-toting woman shot the closest dealer at point blank range before he even knew what hit him. The other two were caught by surprise and raised their hands in defeat.

Without saying a word the women instructed the two remaining dealers to drop their weapons. After the women retrieved the dealers' weapons, one of the women spoke into a tiny mike that was located in a button on her leather jacket.

"Clcar."

At that moment Nettie and Maria walked through the backdoor. They were covered in blood and brain matter.

"Who the fuck let off shots down the hill?" Nettie asked, furiously. No one said a word.

"Well you know it wasn't me, because I don't do guns," Yuming finally answered.

"Look at this shit!" Nettie instructed. "How am I supposed to get this shit cleaned? I can't take this to a cleaner with blood and shit all over it. Y'all bitches gon' pay for this shit. I'm taking it right outta y'all's profit."

Just as the women began to protest, Nettie silenced them by raising her hand and frowning.

"We here to do business," she said, walking over to the table where the product still lay.

"Pack this shit up and let's ride," she said.

Nettie put her finger to her ear, where there was an earpiece pushed down into the canal.

"What?" she asked, speaking into a button pinned to the collar of her coat. "Let's pack this shit up. Somebody heard the shots. Let's move!" she instructed after listening closely to the voice coming through her earpiece.

Nettie had received word, through the earpiece, that a police car was sitting at the security booth at the main entrance of the complex. The information was relayed to her by Little Cash who was positioned on the roof of a house located across the street from the townhouse development. He was the eyes for the crew. He lay on the roof of the house with night vision binoculars to survey the area and keep an eye on the townhouse security.

All three of the dealers, Stacks included, were now seated on the floor. Their hands were taped with masking tape, all except Stacks'. The four women worked expeditiously to gather all the product. When they were finished they vanished out the backdoor and into the night. Nettie held out her hand and asked Maria for one of the two guns she held.

"Are you sure about this, mamí?" Maria asked, surprised. She knew that Nettie had never shot a gun before and she wasn't sure this would be the right time for target practice. Especially when Nettie knew the police could be there any second.

Nettie took the gun from Maria after she gave her a look of disgust. Nettie then turned to the men, sitting there looking like they wanted to shit bricks—all except Stacks. He was hardened to a life of crime, so he knew what time it was. He wasn't afraid to die. He knew that death was part of the game. When you stepped foot into the game, you always had one foot in the grave anyway.

Stacks mean mugged Nettie while she walked over toward the trio. She popped one of the dealers in the head with a bullet and watched his head as it slammed into the wall behind him, splattering it with blood. The blood squirted onto Stacks and the other dealer, Dave. Stacks watched his partner and good friend begin to cry as snot and urine left his body. Nettie laughed at the man.

"You little bitch, crying and shit," she said and then she shot him in the dick and watched him scream and squirm.

This experience gave Nettie an adrenaline rush like no other. She had never felt such a rush, even when she slit someone's throat. She liked the feeling it gave her.

"Come on, mamí, we don't have time for this shit. He making too much noise. We gotta go right now." Maria's accent seemed to be thicker than normal.

Maria stepped up and fired two shots into the man's chest, slumping him and then aimed at Stacks.

"No." Nettie stopped her. "Let him live."

"What, are you crazy? We can't leave no witnesses."

"Trust me I know what I'm doing, plus he won't tell. Will you?" she asked Stacks.

But Stacks didn't say a word. He hocked up spit from his throat and spat it to the floor, looking up at Nettie with the meanest look he could muster.

Nettie laughed and turned to walk toward the back door. She turned back and fired two shots into the wall just above Stacks' head. He ducked and protected his head. Nettie burst into laughter.

"Let's ride," she said and walked out the backdoor.

As Maria was walking out, she heard the unconscious guard grunt, indicating that he was still alive. She shot him in the head and quickly followed behind Nettie.

CHAPTER 18

The clicking sound of a round being chambered was what the teen heard. The hard steel pressed to the back of his head was a good indication that he was being robbed. He carefully raised his hands so he wouldn't alarm the gunman. The robber grabbed a handful of the teen's coat and took him to the side of a house located on N. Sixth Avenue in East Orange. The man was strong and practically dragged the teen with him. He then slammed the teen, face first, into the building's siding, where a knot formed instantly on his forehead. The man then spun the teen and slammed him into the wall again. This time the back of his head felt the force of the blow.

It was well after one a.m. and a much more pleasant night compared to the brutal cold weather they had been having. The streets were mostly deserted as most of the dealers had gone in for the night. That night a release party was jumping off for a famous rapper that grew up in Essex County. Everybody went to the party to show him love as, he too, used to grind on those very streets before he became famous. The eager teen soldier thought about calling it a night because the traffic flow was slow, but he was different from the rest. Greed consumed his mind and he thought that since the rest had left the block, he would make the biggest profit. The last time he counted the grip, he was up to seven hundred and some change. Not bad money for it to be a slow night. Now he wished he hadn't been so greedy and had gone to party instead.

Now, he stood there looking down the barrel of the Glock, hoping and praying that he made it out alive. He had heard about situations like this but had yet to experience one. He remembered right at that moment how he and his boys were just talking about the recent murders. He was loud-mouthed and confident, expressing that if it had been him, he would have handled the situation differently. But now that he was caught up in the actual situation, fear had taken over his body.

"Run ya shit," was all the robber said.

"It's over there," he pointed, barely audible.

The gunman looked in the direction the teen was pointing and then looked back at him. He rammed the nose of the gun into the boy's mouth, causing his gums to bleed.

"Come on, man!" The teen tried to speak as a lone tear fell from his right eye.

"I'm gonna say it again. Run ya shit."

"I swear, man, it's over there in the can sitting by the steps." The muffled sentence came from his bloody lips.

"Where the product at?"

"The product is in the can and the money is in a paper bag inside the drain pipe," the teen cried.

The gunman removed the gun from the boy's mouth

and punched him in the stomach, causing him to lurch over in pain. He spat blood to the ground as he coughed and gagged. The gunman grabbed the teen and slammed him against the building again, but this time he kneed the boy in the nuts. The young teen slid down the wall, sitting on the ground before falling over onto his side, holding his precious jewels. The pain seemed to blind him as he lay there, coughing up blood. The gunman walked over to the drain pipe and removed the paper bag, never taking his eyes off the teen. He then walked over to the can that sat on the side of the steps. He raised what appeared to be a can of Ravioli and examined it. He noticed that the can's top had been carefully cut and replaced. The average person would never have noticed the slight alteration. He then removed the top of the can and pulled out the rolled-up plastic bag.

He shoved everything into his pockets and walked back over to the teen tossing the can to the ground. He stood over the panting boy and began to kick him repeatedly in the face. The teen tried to block his head from receiving the blows as he lay balled in a fetal position.

After stomping the boy unconscious, the gunman proceeded to walk down the street. He wasn't aware that a black Mercedes had driven past while he was putting in work on the teen and now was creeping up behind him as he walked.

When the gunman finally heard the vehicle, he reached inside his coat pocket, placing his hand around the hammer and fingering it. He kept his pace but also listened intently to what was going on behind him, never turning to look. As the vehicle got closer, the driver's side window rolled down.

"Yo, Wild, is that you?" the driver shouted out the window.

Wild whirled around with his arm outstretched the gun locked in position on its target.

"Yo, chill, man. It's me, Nate," the driver said.

Wild squinted his eyes to adjust to the darkness inside the vehicle, trying to focus on the driver.

"Yo man, come on, it's Nate," he said, putting his head out the window a little so that Wild could see his face.

With his hand held steady, Wild lowered the gun as he finally recognized his old friend. A smile came across his lips.

"Nigga, you was almost eatin' dirt," Wild said.

Nate threw the car in park and got out and walked over to Wild. The two shook hands and embraced.

"Yo, nigga, what's up?" Nate asked, excited to see Wild. They both stepped back after releasing their handshake, taking a look at one another.

"Ain't shit going on, man. What's up with you?"

Nate and Wild had known each other since juvenile detention, where they met when Wild was fifteen and Nate was eleven. Wild had been in and out of foster homes and detention and had developed a hardened shell that no one could break. Nate caught a theft charge for stealing cars, so when they met in juvie the two seemed to hit it off lovely. Nate became one of his first friends and they spent almost three years together in juvie. They were then released only to meet back up in Northern State five years later. With this reunion, they became inseparable.

They served their time together, but Nate was due to be released before Wild. Nate told Wild that when he got out he would be put on with a team of getting'-money niggas. Nate promised Wild that when he got out, Nate would make sure that he put him on, too. But when Wild was released, he never returned to those streets where Nate worked. He ventured off to other states and bounced around for more than five years until finally returning to Essex County. Now, he was thirty-nine-years-old and was sticking up young dealers for a living.

"Real talk, man, I saw what you did to little man back there. The first time I rode through, I saw what was going down. But I had this Shorty in the whip and I ain't want her to see what was about to pop off. So when I dropped her off and swung back through, that's when I saw you walking. And don't nobody I know walk like you. I said to myself, 'I'd know that walk from anywhere.'" Nate laughed.

Wild didn't outright laugh, but he did smile. What he was more interested in was where Nate was going with the whole conversation. Wild became defensive again and put his hand in his pocket, resting it on the gun. He would hate to do it, but he would put a bullet in his old friend with the quickness.

"You know I never forgot the bond we had, man. I looked for you for years after I got out, to put you on, like I said. I'm doing a little something with Big Roy right now. Let me put you on with us. That shit right there," Nate said, pointing back down the street where Wild had left the teen unconscious, "that ain't cool, Wild, man. You too old for that life and you need to put your skills to better use. Me and this little squad I run with got something we working on, right now, that's gonna set us up. And, now that I think of it, you just the nigga I need to help me pull off this shit."

Just hearing Big Roy's name was an adrenaline rush for Wild. He was already thinking how he could keep his man Nate close to him so that he could eventually get to Leroy.

"You a'ight, man?" Nate asked, noticing that Wild had a menacing look on his face.

"Yeah. I'm good, man." Wild came back to reality. "Listen, man, I fell off and I gotta do what I gotta do. But now that I ran into you, I know we about to set it off." Wild expressed his gratitude, knowing the real reason he was glad to see Nate.

"I feel you, Wild. We've all fell off a time or two, but those days are over for you. Hop in and let me tell you about a plan that is gonna cake you up big time."

Nate walked toward the car, and Wild followed him. Once inside, Wild admired the leather interior and the sound system Nate had installed.

Before Nate put the car in gear, he turned to Wild.

"Yo, man, just to let you know, *you* was almost a dead man back there."

Wild looked over at Nate with his lips twisted, as if Nate was out of his mind.

"Nigga, how you figure? Listen, Nate, I ain't no square nigga. I had you spotted from the rip. You see the killer dog?" He pulled out the Glock and showed Nate. "This dog right here had already been told to attack." A cocky smirk came across Nate's face.

"You obviously forgot who *I* am, nigga," Nate said.

Nate pushed a button located just under the steering column and Wild looked on in amazement as the armrest on the door panel retracted and out came a Tec-9. Nate looked over at Wild. Wild nodded his head and held out his fist. Nate gave him a pound and the two rode off into the night.

CHAPTER 19

Detective Daniels sat at the desk he hardly occupied. It was covered with files and paperwork he had no intention of looking through. His main objective was to destroy Leroy Jenkins. He seemed to have become obsessed with it. He knew Leroy had most of the city in the palm of his hand, as well as in his pockets. He heard stories of how this man went from a two-bit hustler to a street legend and millionaire, all in the many decades that he walked the earth. He was never jailed or convicted of any crime. There was no way a man could live to see over sixty, living the lifestyle that Leroy did, and never do any jail time. Detective Daniels vowed that if he had to die trying, he would put an end to the amount of corruption that Leroy brought to the city.

As he sat and looked over several notes that he took from some of his reliable street sources, he pondered over the thought of continuing to see Janet. She was becoming quite rambunctious and demanding of his time. His job came first and always had. He was sure that he made that clear to her but to let Janet tell it, he promised her the moon and the stars.

He did love her, though, and toyed with the idea of marrying her. And he did mean what he said to her about things getting better for them. He just didn't know when.

Detective Daniels was thirty-eight-years-old and could be arrogant at times, but he had lived through a lot. After graduating college he jumped from job to job for about seven years, getting nowhere. The thought of joining the force stayed on his mind for a long time before he finally enrolled at the police academy. His father had been a cop and lost his life in the line of duty when Detective Daniels was just fifteen.

One day his father, whose name was Walter, and his partner were in pursuit of a stolen car. In the stolen car were two boys, fourteen- and fifteen-years-old. The vehicle skidded out of control, flipping over three times, and finally found its resting spot wrapped around a tree. The driver of the vehicle was thrown from the car. His neck was broken and he died instantly. However, the young boy that lay trapped in the vehicle was still alive. He had major trauma wounds and Walter was flabbergasted at the sight of the young boy. He fought back tears as he envisioned his own son, who was the same age. He wanted to save the boy's life so that his parents wouldn't suffer the loss of their child.

Walter held the young boy's hand and talked to him while waiting for help to arrive. The boy began to cry and apologize for all that he had done. Several minutes later the young boy died, holding his hand.

Walter was never the same since that day. He talked to Rick, day in and day out, about the streets. He advised him on how to make it in the cruel society in which they lived.

One year later, on the day of the anniversary of the young boys' death, Walter was riding in his cruiser, doing a routine check on the drug-infested streets. His partner was out sick that day, so Walter traveled alone. His captain advised all of his men not to travel alone when working in the high-risk areas, but Walter had a certain amount of respect from the community and the drug pushers alike. The streets loved him and respected him, or so he thought.

He pulled over to the side of the road and double-parked his patrol car. He got out to speak to a favorite resident of his by the name of Mable Wilson. She was an elderly, blind woman who sat on her porch every day of the week, as long as the weather permitted.

Once Walter was finished talking with Mable, he proceeded toward his cruiser when a black Regal skidded around the corner on two wheels, racing up the street toward him. Before Walter could reach the driver's side door to prepare himself for the chase, a hooded man stood up out of the sunroof and filled Walter's body with hollow-point bullets, killing him instantly.

Detective Rick Daniels wasn't the same kid after his father died. He rebelled and buried his sorrows deep inside, looking for a way out. He still attended college, as he felt he owed it to his father. Unfortunately, his mother died a few years after his father and Detective Daniels soon lost his way. They never found the killers that took his fathers life.

Detective Daniels was left alone to live in the shadows of his father. In his second year of college, after his mother's death, he began to use that as an excuse to turn down the wrong path. He became involved in everything from selling drugs and guns to selling stolen goods. You name it and Detective Daniels had done it or had been a part of it. He'd even sampled with a few white college kids on how to manufacture dust, opium, hash and acid.

After a near-death experience when he almost overdosed on heroine, Detective Daniels swore to change his life. As he lay there in the hospital bed with a tube down his throat and nostrils in order to pump his stomach, he dreamt that he saw his father. His father spoke to him about the way he was living his life. He told him how he was heading for destruction. His father told him how his mother was so upset that he had chosen to live the way that he was.

On graduation night, Detective Daniels and the rest of the college campus partied in celebration of no more education. Most of the students didn't know where their next step would put them. But Detective Daniels knew and had since turned his life around and graduated with honors. His goal was to keep the streets clean of the scum that littered it.

The phone began to ring on Detective Daniels's desk. He looked over and lifted the receiver.

"Daniels," he said, listening. "Really? Where are you?"

It was Blist on the other end of the phone.

"I'll be there in a few minutes," Detective Daniels said, slamming down the phone and quickly getting up from his desk.

CHAPTER 20

Detective Daniels walked into the coffee shop and saw Blist sitting at the rear table. Blist looked up to meet his stare. Detective Daniels walked over to the table and sat in the chair.

"What's so important, Dave?"

"Rick, I got a break in the case of the murders down at the cemetery several months ago." Blist took a sip of his coffee.

"Yeah, whatchu got?" Detective Daniels asked eagerly.

"We got a partial print."

"That's big," Detective Daniel smiled.

"Yeah I know,"

"So why you couldn't tell me this over the phone?"

"Well I wanted to sit and talk with you for a minute. You need to relax sometimes," Blist said.

"I will relax later, right now I got cases to solve." Detective Daniels stood and walked out of the coffee shop.

Blist held his head low, looking into his coffee cup.

-⊲⇒-⊲⇒-⊲⇒-

Detective Daniels called down to the station to speak with Sam. He was a finger print expert and if you got an inch of a print, Sam would get the rest.

"What's up, Rick? What can I do for you?" Sam asked.

"What's going on, my friend?" Detective Daniels greeted him over the phone.

"You know, same ol', same ol'. Shifting papers." He laughed.

"Yeah, I hear ya. I need a favor from you, my friend," Detective Daniels said.

"You don't even have to ask. Anything for you, Rick."

"I need to get the file on the cemetery murder case I'm working on. New evidence just came in and they got a partial fingerprint. Sam I need you to handle this one. See if you can come up with something as soon as possible." Detective Daniels said.

"You know I gotcha' back, Rick."

"Call me as soon as you get the results."

Detective Daniels drove with a smile on his face; this could be the big break he needed.

CHAPTER 21

"**B**ig Roy, we got a problem," Dak said, looking at him through the rearview mirror. Dak placed his cell phone on the seat next to him and waited for a response from Leroy.

Leroy blew smoke from his cigar into the air.

"I don't have problems, Dak." He looked at Dak.

"The main stash house in the development was robbed early this morning and four of our security men are dead. All of the lead men for Stacks' team are dead," he said.

Leroy didn't say a word. He kept his eyes focused on the scenery as Dak drove.

"The two men left from the security team seem to think it was an inside job. Stacks was the only one left standing. That's why they think he may have had something to do with it. But then again, they said he sounded on the up and up. He's still local and tryna find out what went down from the streets himself. But it just ain't adding up," Dak said, realizing Leroy was in a zone. "The police released him for lack of evidence after he cried victim. They questioned him for hours but he didn't buck, so they realized he didn't know anything or wasn't snitching. There wasn't any product left in the house either." Dak waited for a response.

He'd seen this side of Leroy many times. He knew from experience that when Leroy was silent, he was in deep thought, and most times that meant trouble.

Leroy chuckled under his breath and continued to puff on his cigar.

"So muthafuckas wanna fuck with mine." Leroy continued to chuckle. "The way I see it, the coach is responsible for the team's losses, and I don't give a shit what them niggas say. I am the coach and owner of this team. I am being looked at like a coach who can't get his team to be winners. If a nigga got balls big enough to take from me, then that muthafucka better be ready for me when I bring the heat," Leroy said in a calm, low voice. This was the same demeanor that Ishmael had carried himself. Obviously, that was one gene Ishmael shared with his father. There was always the calm before the storm and, in Leroy's mind, it was about to be a hell of a monsoon.

"Get in touch with Nate and the rest of them little niggas. Tell them we got a sho-nuff big job for them that's gonna feed their bellies full. They claim they still hungry. Well, if they do this job right, they ain't gonna need to eat for months," he said, referring to Nate and the others as he sucked deeply on the wet end of the cigar.

A half-hour later, Nate, Dice, and Click were walking into the pool hall. Big Dak took them into the office to see Leroy.

"Sit down, fellas," Leroy said.

The trio looked at each other as they realized that Leroy's

demeanor was completely different from what they had ever seen. He looked almost demonic. They all took their seats and gave him their undivided attention.

"Somebody's missing," Leroy said.

"Yeah, Big Roy. Cash is not here," Nate spoke up.

"So, where he at?"

"We don't know. I think he might be home. He got a sick mother," Nate said, reaching, not knowing where Cash had disappeared to. "What's up, Big Roy?"

Leroy sat there staring at Nate before he spoke.

"The kid don't have a jack?"

"Yeah, he got one, but we ain't try to reach out to him. Big Roy, he ain't no problem. Actually, we ya mans right now. We the ones that put in the serious work." Nate tried to convince Leroy that Little Cash was obsolete at that point in time.

Leroy nodded his head with his mouth in an upside-down smile.

"One of my main sets was hit early this morning. Four of my men were killed and four lieutenants were killed. There's one out there who was left standing. In my mind, I know he had something to do with it. I just learned he has now taken flight. I want him found and I want my product back. He will have to resurface sooner or later, and when he does, I want his head sitting on the mantel over my fireplace," Leroy said, pointing toward the fireplace for emphasis. "You bring me my product *and* any money back and all of you will be rewarded heavily. Ya dig?"

"Who we talking about, Roy?" Nate asked.

"Stacks. You know him?" Nate looked at the others and

then back to Leroy.

"Who don't know 'im?"

"Good," Leroy said.

"We got this on lock, Big Roy," Nate said, standing to his feet. "If he's breathing, he can be found. Niggas like him can't keep their mouth shut so, when he opens it, I'ma put something in it." Nate stood there, looking stone-faced.

"Serve that nigga," Dak said.

Leroy looked at Nate and smirked. He was kinda feeling Nate. He really never noticed it before because he just dealt with them on the strength of Ishmael. But the more he came in contact with Nate, the more he saw the potential he had.

He nodded his head at Nate and Nate threw up his head at Leroy. It was like the two men could read each other as they locked eyes. Nate turned to Dice and Click, giving them a look, and began to walk toward the door. The two men followed Nate's lead and walked out of Leroy's office.

CHAPTER 22

Little Cash sat at the table in Maria's kitchen. He was bagging up the product they lifted off Leroy. Nettie was sitting at the table with Little Cash, watching him intently. She was being trained on how to break the product down and package it into the different types of weight for distribution. Maria was standing over the sink, washing dishes from the meal she had cooked for them not long ago.

"So, Nette, who you gonna get to pump this shit?" Little Cash asked. Nettie looked at him sideways.

"What do you mean? We gonna flip this shit."

"Naw, Nette." Little Cash shook his head.

"No? What are you tryna say, Cash?"

"Nette, we just lifted this shit from Big Roy. I work for Big Roy. Do you honestly think I'ma sling this shit right under his nose when I'm supposed to be a part of his security? That nigga will body me in a heart beat. Naw, fam, I ain't going out like that." He shook his head.

"Well, then, the ladies will have to do it," Nettie responded. Maria whirled around, looking at Nettie.

"What? Oh no, mamí, you got the game fucked up. I

dance. I don't know nothing about selling drugs." She sounded mad.

"Word," Little Cash butted in. "I ain't tryna knock ya hustle Nett, but I don't think that would be a good idea, either. I'm sayin' tho', y'all ladies are some hellish hit men, but I don't think slingin' is y'all's style."

"OK, so what the hell is we supposed to do with all this shit, if none of us are going to push it?" Nettie wanted to know.

"What you need to do is let me drop the word to Nate and the rest, letting them know we got our own shit up and running. I'm sure once they see how much work we got, they would be down. We could get them to help recruit some runners and roll from there."

"Yeah, but you don't think that Nate and them won't know that this is Leroy's shit?" Nettie asked.

"Naw, Nettie. They wouldn't know because they security. See, I know a lot about the product end of it more than I know anything about puttin' a nigga to sleep. That just ain't me. I mean, if I had to get down, then I would. But I prefer to get money this way," he said, pointing at the dope that was piled onto the table.

"So what you saying we do, Cash?"

"We need to recruit some young hungry thugs, like I said."

"Well, then, you need to handle that part, because all I'm concerned about right now is gettin' money. My plan is to keep sticking Big Roy for his shit until I eliminate his ass all together."

Little Cash just looked at Nettie like she was crazy. But he really believed she would do it, especially after seeing her in action the other night.

-◈-◈-◈-

Later that night

Nettie sat at the bar at Bodilicious. She was having a drink, talking with the bartender, and waiting for Maria to finish up. In walked Nate and Wild. They sat at the other end of the bar.

Nettie spotted Nate, got off the bar stool and sashayed over to them. She tapped Nate on the shoulder from behind. Nate and Wild both turned around. Wild couldn't believe his eyes. It was her, the gorgeous woman he'd seen the last time he was in the club.

"What's up, Nate?" Nettie smiled.

"What's good, ma?" Nate embraced her.

Wild sat, awestruck, watching the two interact. It had been many years since a woman had him geeking the way that he was now.

Nate released Nettie and immediately introduced her to Wild. A side of Wild that no one had ever seen surfaced. He was suddenly the perfect gentleman.

He could've charmed the pants right off Nettie, standing there in the club. The three talked and drank. When Maria finished her set she walked over to Nettie.

"Hey, mamí, I'm ready now," Maria interrupted.

"Maria, see if you can catch a ride home. I'll see you later."

Maria saw stars. She was enraged with Nettie blowing her off like that and she stormed out of the club.

A few more drinks of the truth serum and Nettie had told them about her plan to get a security team together and recruit some runners for her newfound career.

"So you doing it big, huh, Nette?" Nate asked.

"A little something, you know."

"I admire a woman who knows what she wants and goes out to get it," Wild added, staring deep into her eyes.

"So when you ready to jump start this shit, Nettie?" Nate asked.

"Like yesterday, Nate. I got a shit load of coke and dope. Most of it has already been bagged up. I need some clients to buy weight, too."

"Oh, so you ballin' out like that?" Nate asked.

"I told you, I'm doing a little something-something."

"Oh, a'ight, I feel you. OK, this is what I'm gonna do for you. I'll put Dice and Click on it to recruit some young thoroughbreds. We'll get you some blocks set up to get them started, and I'll keep my ear to the street to get you some cats to buy weight off of you. Now you know Big Roy pretty much got this city on lock," he told her.

If looks could kill, then Nate would have been a dead man. Just the mention of Leroy's name did something to Nettie. Both Nate and Wild caught that look and looked at each other.

"I take it you're not feeling Big Roy?" Wild asked. Nettie looked at Wild and smiled.

"What would give you that idea?" she asked.

"Well, the look on your face for one."

Nettie laughed in a sexy way and placed her hand on Wild's shoulder for emphasis.

"It's just that everybody is sweating' Big Roy's around here and, frankly, I ain't feeling it. He ain't the only dude that can be on the come-up."

"True, true," Wild agreed.

"A'ight then, let me get ya number and I'll hit you back," Nate said.

Nettie called out her number to Nate as he put it in his cell phone. He kissed Nettie on the cheek and gave Wild a pound, then left the club.

"So, Mr. Wild, what kind of a name is that?"

"It's something that kinda stuck with me since I was young." He smiled.

The two continued to talk until the club closed down for the night.

CHAPTER 23

Word on the streets was that Leroy thought Stacks had something to do with the robbery of the stash house. Stacks knew what type of man Leroy was. He, too, would have thought the same thing, had the shoe been on the other foot. He was the only one who survived the massacre, and without a scratch on him. Why would they leave him alive to take the fall? Little did he know that was Nettie's plan. She wanted Leroy to think his own team lifted the product, therefore taking any possible suspicion off of them. He had to get up outta Dodge cause there had to be a bounty on his head by now. Stacks went underground the day after the robbery. That was when word got out that Leroy was looking for him. There was no way in his mind that he would even think about having a sit-down with Leroy to clear his name. His name was already dirt when Leroy found out he was the only one survived when his crew members and his security team were all dead.

Stacks was chilling at the crib of a chick he twisted out from time to time. She lived in the basement apartment on William Street in East Orange. Her name was Daleena and she had nothing but love for Stacks. Although he only stopped by from time to time to run up in her, bust off, and roll out, she still loved him. She would pretty much do anything for him and he knew it. So he took this opportunity to lay low with her, being that no one knew about her. Or so he thought. He wanted to wait until Daleena was scheduled to leave town to head south to see her children—ages three and four—who were staying with Daleena's mother until she was able to finish up her last semester of school.

Daleena didn't have much, but what she had was neat and clean. She worked at the local supermarket by day and went to school for business management by night. Daleena was determined to finish school to better her life for her and her children. Although she lived in low-income housing, she still managed to keep her head up and keep her goals in sight.

Stacks had planned to catch a ride with Daleena when her aunt came to pick her up for the trip south in a week. He planned to take his stash and start a new life in the South.

Stacks lay there on his back, looking over at the TV. *Judge Mathis* was on and he laughed occasionally at the comical cases. The door to the apartment squeaked heavily as it opened. In walked Daleena several seconds later.

"You ain't working today?" he asked her, not looking her way.

"I don't feel so well. My stomach is nauseous," she said, sitting on the bed.

"Fix me a sandwich right quick," he said with no feeling.

"Stacks, didn't you hear me tell you that I am not feeling well? I need to lay down. I feel dizzy right now." She lay down on the bed next to him.

"Damn, a man can't even get a sandwich 'round this muthafucka. I swear, you lazy as hell. You don't half cook now and all I'm asking for is a sandwich," he complained.

"Stacks, I think I'm pregnant."

"What? By who?" he asked, sitting up on the bed and looking at her.

Daleena opened her eyes and looked at him with disbelief.

"Are you seriously asking me who the father of this baby is?" she asked, rubbing her stomach.

"Did I stutter?"

She sucked her teeth and willed herself to get up off the bed. She ran into the bathroom, barely making it to the toilet before she vomited. Ten minutes later she walked into the room. Daleena knew she was pregnant by Stacks from when he came over the last time, two months prior. She tried to contact him but he never returned her calls.

"I'm going to the store to get me a ginger ale and some crackers. Do you want anything?"

"Yeah. How about that sandwich I asked you to make me?"

"Stacks, just give me some money, please," she stated, feeling really irritated with him. She thought he was becoming very arrogant and aggressive. Or was he always like that and she was too dick whooped and loving his street status to realize it? In any case, he was getting on her last nerve the last couple of days. Stacks reached into his pocket and balled up a twenty and threw it at her.

Daleena picked up the money and walked out of the apartment and down the street, heading for the corner store. She walked past a Dodge mini-van that was parked on the corner. Just as she passed the van the doors opened, startling her, and two men got out.

"How you doing, beautiful?" one of the men asked.

Daleena just smiled and kept walking.

The two men headed toward the apartment and entered into the basement's hallway.

Back inside the apartment, Stacks continued to laugh at *Judge Mathis's* antics as he tried to help the oddball couple that stood before him, beefing over who ate up all the food in the house. The beef ultimately turned into an argument that turned into a fight, which damaged the apartment they shared.

A knock came at the door. Stacks didn't budge. He never answered the door since no one knew he was there and Daleena had a key. The knock came again, as if the visitor knew someone was in the house.

Stacks raised up off the bed and looked in the direction of the hallway, as if he had super powers to see through the thick, wood door. When he turned his attention back to the TV, he spotted Daleena's keys on the dresser.

"Shit," he said, realizing she forgot her keys and was coming back to get them, which meant he had to get up off the bed to take them to her.

He scooped the keys off the dresser and headed toward the door.

He never looked in the peephole, but instead he snatched the door open, ready to bust her in her grill for making him get up from his comfortable spot on the bed.

He opened the door only to meet the butt end of a Glock to his forehead splitting the skin. Stacks stumbled backward in a dizzy haze, trying to keep his balance. Nate and Dice walked into the small apartment and closed the door behind them. They had left Click in the van as a lookout. Dice grabbed Stacks before he could fall to the floor. He placed him into a chair that sat at the kitchen table. Stacks looked up at the two intruders with blurred vision. Both men stood there staring down at him, neither of them uttering a word. When Stacks was able to get his vision in check, he realized what time it was. The blood ran down his face, leaving red river trails on the way to his chin before dropping onto his shirt.

"Yo, man, I ain't do it," he protested.

"Ain't nobody ask you nothing," Nate said.

"You already bitch'n up, nigga," Dice added.

"Where the loot and product at?" Nate asked him.

"I told you, I ain't do it. Somebody set me up," Stacks tried to explain.

"One more time," Nate said, obviously not impressed with the answer he received. "Where the shit at?"

"I told you—" Stacks never finished his sentence before Dice hit him again with the gun.. Stacks' nose was broken and he knew it by the sound that it made that still echoed in his head.

Blood gushed from the open skin on top of his nose and from his nostrils. Dice then hit him in his stomach and Stacks doubled over, coughing up blood and spitting it to the floor.

The door to the apartment opened and Daleena appeared. She dropped her bag to the floor. The plastic bottle of ginger ale hit the floor with a loud thud. The bottle spun around spitting soda from the broken top. Nate and Dice whirled around to meet her with their guns pointing her way. Dice capped off and hit her in the stomach with a round, sending her flying back out into the hallway. Nate looked at him and shook his head.

"What, man? Shit, I thought the bitch was shooting at us."

Click was outside talking to a girl and never saw Daleena walk past him, so there was no warning.

Nate turned his attention to Stacks, knowing they had to finish the job before someone called the police. He also knew that if they came back with money or the product, then they would get a bonus in pay from Leroy.

"You wanna live, nigga, or do you want to end up like ya bitch?" he grilled Stacks.

"Yo, man, she was pregnant, man. You killed my seed," Stacks said, looking out into the hallway where Daleena distorted body lay, twisted.

Nate realized that he wasn't going to get anything out of Stacks, so he shot him in the head twice. He and Dice proceeded to search the apartment as fast as they could and kept coming up empty-handed. They never found Stacks' stash that he had hidden. The money was taped to the bottom of the TV.

CHAPTER 24

A day later

Nate met Leroy at the Halal restaurant where he had the whole back section to himself. He sat there alone and ate while Dak and two other men stood with watchful eyes.

After Nate walked into the restaurant, he headed straight for Leroy. Dak stopped him and patted him down, removing his nine-millimeter.

"You'll get this back when you're done," Dak said and stepped aside.

"Have a seat, son," Leroy instructed as he sucked the meat off a smothered turkey wing.

Nate took a seat in front of him and waited for Leroy to speak.

"I like you, Nate," Leroy said, sucking his greasy fingers. "You seem to be a real thorough cat."

Nate simply nodded his head, all the while thinking how getting next to Leroy might be easier than he thought. He could tell that Leroy was starting to trust him, which was exactly what he needed him to do.

"You hungry?"

"I'm good, Roy." Nate declined the offer.

"So, what's up with Stacks?"

"Oh, you ain't heard?" Nate asked, surprised. He thought Leroy had the jump on everything.

In fact, Nate couldn't get a sit-down with Leroy the same day to tell him what happened. So he figured Leroy already knew when he called him to the restaurant. Dak, head of security was the one who paid Nate for the job. Leroy already knew, but he wanted to hear it from Nate.

"Ya boy Stacks should be in the morgue on ice by now. Him, his girl, and their unborn seed," Nate said with no remorse.

"Dayum." Leroy looked surprised. "You heartless just like I like 'em. That's a job well done. What you bring back?"

"There was no loot or product there," Nate responded.

"Where the product?" Leroy never looked up. He just kept eating.

"Dunno. He wouldn't buck, so we just did him."

Leroy took a sip of his sweet tea and looked at Nate for what seemed like an eternity. But Nate didn't blink. He held Leroy's stare.

Nate was starting to see right through Leroy. He felt that if Leroy didn't have security around him 24/7, he wouldn't be the man that he was.

Leroy began to suck on his teeth in an attempt to remove the food from between them.

"A'ight, young blood, I'm feeling you. Look here, I got another job for you and ya boys. I got a flock of them birds coming in a couple of weeks. You think you can handle the delivery?"

Nate gave a confident smirk. "No doubt, Roy."

Nate couldn't believe the bullshit job Leroy was asking if he could handle. He was actually quite insulted.

"Cool. I'll have somebody get back to you later."

With that said, Leroy began to eat again. Nate took that as his cue and stood to leave.

He walked over to Dak, who was already waiting with Nate's gun in his hand. Nate walked out of the restaurant and over to his car, where Wild sat in the passenger's seat.

"So, what's up?" Wild asked.

"That nigga tripping. He just gave me a bullshit delivery boy job."

"What's the job?" Wild asked.

"He got a load of them thangs coming in and he wants me to deliver them to one of his spots."

Wild sat, heavy in thought, while Nate continued to vent.

"Leroy got three of his boys in there with him. I know that's easy play for you and me to handle," Nate said, looking over at Wild. "I say we go back in there and waste all of them, Leroy included."

"Naw, Nate. Slow ya roll, fam. This could play to our advantage. You hold the key to the keys. You feel me?" Wild looked over at Nate referring to the kilo's of Cocaine that was being delivered.

Nate looked at Wild with a smirk on his face as he started the car and pulled off.

CHAPTER 25

It was a Thursday and an unusual day. It was sixty-five degrees and it felt like spring, although it was November. The kids all filed out of the high school at about twelve thirty p.m. that day after a half day of classes. Some of the young teens conversed in front of the school, while others began their walks to their destinations. Some piled into cars that were waiting or the cars that seniors with licenses drove. A black Audi 600 sat across the street. The owner of the vehicle was Dice. He leaned on the front of the car, with his arms were folded across his chest while an iced-out Rolex watch sparkled in the sunlight.

Click sat in the passenger's seat. He had the seat laid way back with his foot, sporting Uptowns, resting partially out the window. A peach-flavored Switzer blunt filled with 'dro clung to his lip.

Dice watched barely legal teenage girls as they walked by him, adding more swing to their hips than they needed. He frolicked with a few of them, toying with their minds until he spotted the victim he had come to see. His face suddenly became serious and he dismissed the girls. Out of the double doors walked TJ. He walked down to the sidewalk and began his journey home, heading toward Dice.

"What up, TJ?" Dice asked as the young boy walked toward him.

TJ just looked at Dice and threw his head up in acknowledgement.

"Yo, you need a ride?"

"Naw, I'm good," TJ said as he strolled by Dice.

"A-Yo, let me holla at you for a minute," Dice called out to him.

TJ stopped and hesitantly turned around. He looked up at Click, who had just gotten out of the car and was now walking up next to Dice.

"C'mere, man, ain't nobody gon' do nothing to ya," Dice assured him.

Just then Tyler came walking up and stood next to TJ, as if he smelled beef and was coming to his boy's rescue.

Dice laughed and looked over at Click as he was looking the young, boy up and down.

"Look at this clown," Click said to Dice. "Yo, man, whatchu 'bout to do, standing there with yo' chest on swole?" Click purposely raised the colored long john shirt he sported under the jogging suit so that the butt end of his arsenal would show.

"Yo, is that a four-five?" Tyler's front disappeared as soon as he saw the weapon. "Yo, I ain't never seen one up close before." He began to walk over to Click when TJ grabbed him by the arm and began pulling him away from the two men.

Just as they reached the corner, TJ pushed Tyler up against the building.

"Tyler, what is wrong with you, man? Are you crazy?"

"What, TJ? What did I do?"

"Man, you can't go around acting like you soft. Do you know who those cats are?"

"No, but I know they was packin' heat. Besides, when I saw you talking to them, I thought maybe you might have known them anyway," Tyler stated, as naïve as they come.

"Tyler, man, let me explain something to you. If you don't get you some balls, and I mean real soon, these streets are going to eat you alive. These cats out here ain't playin' around. You claim you love the street life and everything that comes with it. But you ain't gonna make it if niggas think you a punk. I ain't gonna be around you all the time to save your ass if you get into some shit." TJ walked off, leaving Tyler dumbfounded.

TJ walked ahead of Tyler and concentrated on the lines that separated each block of cement as he walked. He was in deep thought, as usual. At one time he had toyed with the idea of putting in work. But he was never impressed with that type of lifestyle, although he had been brought up around it all of his life. He had seen what it had done to people in his life—his mother mainly—and he vowed never to fall into that melting pot of street life. Just recently he decided to attend school regularly, get his grades on point. He planned to further his education by graduating and studying law. TJ wanted to make sure that children whose parents were murdered would never have to feel what he was feeling. He felt emptiness not only from losing the only person who loved him and his sister unconditionally, but also from not being able to put his mother's soul to rest by finding her killer.

TJ knew that he would never be able to go to a good college because of the financial situation with his grandmother. He also knew that if he didn't find a way to begin saving money for college, he might end up like most of the kids living in the hood.

He came back to reality and realized that Tyler was not walking beside him. He turned around to look behind him and saw a very sad Tyler, trailing far behind.

"Come on, Tyler, man." TJ stopped and waited for him.

"I'm sorry, TJ. I messed up, right?" Tyler looked at him with sadness covering his face.

"No, it's not that you messed up, Tyler, it's . . . never mind," TJ said as they turned and began their walk home, shoulder to shoulder.

Later that night, after the boys finished their homework, they were sitting in their usual spot on TJ's porch. It was after six PM and already dark. The same Audi 600 from the school pulled up in front of the house.

"Yo, TJ, ain't that the cats who was rappin' to you in front of the school?" Tyler asked.

TJ looked at the car and didn't say a word. He was wondering how they knew where he lived.

Dice and Click got out of the car.

"What's up, TJ?" Click asked as he leaned on the vehicle.

Dice was already leaning on the door with his arms folded across his chest.

TJ didn't say a word. He just looked at them with a

serious face. Both men approached the porch. Click leaned against the banister and Dice put one foot on the first step.

"What's crackin', fellas?" Tyler sounded corny, and Dice began to laugh.

"I like you, man. What's your name?" Dice asked.

"It's Tyler, but my peeps call me T-Y," he stated proudly.

TJ looked over at his friend and wished they were inside, instead of where they were.

Dice and Click burst into laughter. Tyler joined in, not knowing they were clowning him.

"Yo, TJ, what you been up to, man?" Dice asked.

TJ just shook his head.

"You got some money in ya pockets, man?" Dice continued to question him.

"Hell no, he ain't got no loot. Look at his footwear. How you walking 'round here, lookin' busted?" Click cracked.

"Yo, man, chill," Dice warned after seeing the look on TJ's face that told him the boy was embarrassed.

"Listen, TJ, I got a way you can make some serious ends. I know you don't want to keep looking like you do."

TJ didn't say a word. He already knew where Dice was going with the conversation. But Tyler had no clue.

"I want to make some dough. Can I get a piece?" Tyler asked.

"Naw, fam, you ain't built for this," Dice said, shaking his head. "But my man right here is. So what's up, TJ? You wanna make some money or not?"

TJ still didn't answer. He just stared seriously at Dice, eyeballing him.

"What you want him to do?" Tyler asked, still eager.

"We need him to hand out packages," Click said, still clowning Tyler.

"I can do that. That's easy. Why can't I get down?" Tyler asked.

Click began to laugh again. Dice kept staring at TJ.

"Listen, little man, you can make a lot of cash. I know its some things you would like to buy. I know your little sister might want some new shit, too."

"Come on, man. TJ, that's easy money we can make. I mean, you can make, but I can help you if you like," Tyler tried to reason.

TJ just sat in thought, now staring at the ground. He really did need some new clothes, and so did his sister. He could really help his grandmother out with the extra money coming in. Not to mention the fact that he could save his money for college.

"So what happens when we get locked-up?" TJ finally asked.

"You just handing out packages. How you gonna get popped for doing that?" Tyler asked.

"Yo, little man, chill," Dice warned Tyler.

"Don't worry about that. We got you if you get picked up," Click added.

"Yeah. We take care of our own, plus ya moms was good peoples," Dice said.

"I'll do it if you put my man right here on, too." TJ looked at Dice.

Dice turned and looked at Click.

"I don't know, man," Click said to Dice. "The boy seems as dumb as a box of rocks to me but it's your call," Click said, walking back over to the car.

Dice stood there for a minute, contemplating the move. He looked at Tyler.

"Yo, do you know what you about to get into?" he asked Tyler.

"Yeah. You want us to hand out packages."

"It's not just handing them out, man. Wait, do you know what kind of packages?"

"I'll put him down," TJ spoke up.

"Yeah, you better because if he fuck up any of the work, it's yo' ass I'm coming after." Dice pointed to TJ.

"I ain't gonna fuck up, man," Tyler said.

"Yeah, a'ight. I'll get back up with you with the work tomorrow." Dice walked away, not sure if he had made the right move.

CHAPTER 26

Little Cash walked up the steps to Nate's apartment on the first floor of a two-family house. He rang the bell and waited for an answer. Finally Nate opened the door and let him in, not saying a word. Little Cash walked in with confidence because he knew he was coming to rub in Nate's face how he was starting his own crew to put in work. If they wanted in, they needed to come through him.

When he walked into the living room, he saw Dice and Click lounging around, blowing trees. There were three stacks of money sitting on the table in front of them.

"Yo, nigga, where you been?" Dice asked.

"I been doin' what I do," a cocky Little Cash said.

"Yeah, like what?" Click asked, passing the blunt over to Dice.

"Oh, I'm 'bout to tell y'all niggas now." Little Cash sat on one of the recliners.

"You still never answered the question," Nate said.

"What question?" Little Cash asked.

"Where you been, nigga?" Nate asked, much louder this time.

"I told you, I been out getting shit poppin'. Why? What's up, Nate?" Little Cash challenged. "You soundin' real hostile and shit. Did I do something to you?"

"Hell, yeah, you did. We had to swing by Big Roy's to do a job and he asked about you. He wasn't feelin' that yo dumb ass was MIA," Nate said while pointing at Little Cash.

"So what you saying? Big Roy don't trust me or some shit?"

"I don't know what Big Roy thinking. All I know is that I put my ass on the line for you. But you know what? Thanks for getting low, because we got paid to do a job and we didn't have to split it four ways," Nate said, referring to the stacks of money on the table.

Little Cash was heated at first and then he remembered why he came by Nate's house. He was about to blow their shit out of the water. He knew what he was about to tell them would have them beggin' to get put on, or so he thought.

"Yeah, well, that ain't shit right there." He pointed to the money. "I'm doing bigger things than that nickel-and-dime shit. Me and Nett got our own shit started and trust we gon' be making major dough," Little Cash said with confidence.

"Nett?" Nate asked.

"Yeah, fam, Nettie from the strip joint. I ran into her and she asked me to get down with her. She copped a boatload of shit and I am the brains behind getting the product off." Little Cash mean-mugged Nate with confidence.

Nate looked at Dice and Click. They were already looking at him and then they all turned to look at Little Cash.

Dice burst into laughter first and then the rest followed. They laughed for the better part of five minutes. Little Cash just sat there, looking at them and wondering if they thought he was bullshitting.

"Yo, man,"—Nate tried to catch his breath—"you ain't running shit with Nettie. If anything, I'm running security and you gonna take your direction from me, son."

"Since when you capable of running anything? For real, man. Whatever you on, you need to stop smoking it, 'cause it's got ya' head all fucked up." Click chuckled.

"Yeah, a'ight, you ain't gotta believe me. You'll see. Now if y'all niggas want to get down, then just let me know and I'll put a bug in Nettie's ear and we can go from there." Little Cash was serious.

They all started laughing again. This really pissed off Little Cash because they were taking him for a joke.

"What the fuck is so funny?" he shouted.

"You, nigga," Click said, pointing at Little Cash.

"Yo, Cash, man, didn't you hear what I said? I said, if anything, you gonna have to take your direction from me. Yo, son, I *been* spoke to Nettie and she already put us on. Dice and Click already started recruiting to get rid of the packages and Wild is getting customers to buy the weight. Now if you keep your hands out yo' pants, whackin' off your shit of long enough, you would know that by now." Nate laughed.

"What?" Little Cash couldn't believe his ears. Why would Nettie go against the grain and put them on, when he clearly told her he would do it? Now he looked like a sucker in front of them and, once again, incapable of doing anything on his own.

Little Cash was real tired of them belittling him and putting him down. He was tired of Nate taking all the credit for work that he did, while Dice and Click were his flunkies, sucking his dick when needed. He stood and walked out of the apartment, listening to their laughter fade behind him.

Once outside, he walked down the street and around the corner to the bodega. He stepped inside and purchased a soda. He came back outside and pulled out his cell phone from his jeans' pocket. He dialed Nettie's cell phone number. She answered quickly.

"What's up, Nett?" Little Cash asked.

Nettie noticed the slight attitude in his voice.

"What's good, Cash?"

"You tell me."

"I'm detecting from ya voice that you got a problem with me." She was on the defensive.

"Yeah, I do. What's up with telling Nate and them 'bout coming on with us?"

"Hold up. And your problem is what?" Nettie asked, listening to what Little Cash had just said.

"Nett, I think that was some fucked-up and shady shit you pulled. We talked about this, and I told you I was gonna tell them niggas."

"Cash, what difference does it make? I saw them at the club, so I just told them. Stop tripping. It ain't that serious."

"Yeah, a'ight, Nett. It's like that?" he asked, surprised that Nettie would do him dirty.

"Cash, please, okay? You blowin' shit up. You still got ya spot. So, stop beatin' me over the head with the bullshit, a'ight?" she asked, getting aggravated.

Little Cash felt punked. "Yeah. A'ight," he said.

"We on our way, baby boy, so hold ya head, a'ight?" Nettie

said, trying to convince him that he was still very much apart of the team.

"No doubt." He didn't sound convinced.

"A'ight, I'll hit you later."

"One!" Little Cash disconnected the call.

CHAPTER 27

Nettie walked into the apartment at three a.m. for the second night in a row. Maria lay in bed, appearing to be asleep, but she was far from asleep. Nettie went into the bathroom. Once she came out, she climbed into bed.

"So this how it's gonna be, Netta?" Maria asked.

"Like how, Maria?"

"Like this." She turned to face Nettie. "This right here. You coming and going as you please."

"Maria, I'm grown. I do what I want to do. Don't start. Obviously you didn't hear me when I told you that everything I do is for us."

"Oh, you mean like screwing men?" Maria asked sarcastically.

"Yes, like fucking men." Nettie didn't sugarcoat her answer. "I told you I will do some things you may not like. So what's ya problem? I go both ways, Maria, and you knew that from the rip. Miss me with the bullshit, okay?" Nettie sat up.

"Oh, okay, mamí, that's how it is, huh? I bust my ass for you and you do me like this?" Her accent thickened.

"Maria, come on! You can't be serious? I can't do this with you right now. I'm out here trying to get this thing off the ground, and you bending my ear back with the bullshit. No, Maria, I don't need this right now. What I need is for you to be that down bitch you claim you are. What's up with that?"

"I am that down chick, Netta. But I feel like you kicking me to the curb. I don't feel like I am part of the team," Maria said sincerely. Nettie fell back onto the bed.

"Get ya mind right, Maria, seriously. We about to kick this thing into overdrive and I need you focused. We *need* those dudes I was kicking it to. They some real cats. They're cut from a different cloth. Don't start tripping. It's all gonna work out." With that said, Nettie turned her back to Maria.

Maria looked at her for a few minutes longer and then she lay back down.

The next morning

Maria walked down the hallway of the apartment building after returning from the grocery store. She had gotten up early because she couldn't sleep. She walked into the apartment, kicked the door shut behind her and headed through the living room into the kitchen.

When she got to the kitchen she screamed and dropped both grocery bags to the kitchen floor. Meat turned around when he heard her scream. Maria grabbed a knife from the knife caddy that sat on the counter and charged at Meat.

He grabbed her by the arms to keep her at bay.

"Maria! Chill out!" Nettie came running into the kitchen

to intervene. "This is my boy, Meat!"

Maria stood there, breathing hard, staring at the huge man.

"You remember I told you I saw him the other day?"

"No, I don't." Maria continued to breathe heavily. "What is he doing here?"

"He is going to be a part of the team. Now calm down!"

Maria relaxed her arms and Meat removed the large butcher knife from her right hand. She backed away from him, clearly showing that she was bothered by his excess skin. Meat placed the knife on the table and shoved his hands into his pants pockets. Meat just stared at Maria, making her feel uncomfortable. But to him, she was beautiful.

"Netta, can I talk to you?" Maria asked and left the kitchen without waiting for a reply.

"Did you get you something to drink?" Nettie turned to Meat.

He shook his head.

"Don't worry about her. I'll talk to her," Nettie told him. "Go 'head and get you something to drink and I'll be back."

Meat had called Nettie a little after seven that morning. She told him to come over and she would fill him in on what she needed from him. Meat was out getting his morning paper and was in the area, so he had arrived quickly. When he got there, Nettie hadn't gotten dressed yet, underestimating his arrival time. Once in the apartment he asked her for something to drink. Nettie told him he was welcome to whatever was in the refrigerator. She went into the bedroom to get dressed and then Maria came home and found him in the kitchen.

"Netta, who is that?" Maria asked before Nettie could close the bedroom door.

"That's Meat, Maria." She walked over to the dresser and removed a T-shirt.

"That's not telling me anything." Maria stood with her hands on her wide hips.

Nettie let her robe drop to the floor. She put on her T-shirt and proceeded to the closet, grabbing a pair of jeans from a hanger.

"Maria, what do you want from me?" Nettie finally asked.

"I want to know who he is and why he is here."

"I told you already. I ain't gonna keep repeating myself, and I damn sure ain't know I had to report to you." She pulled the jeans up over her onion.

"No creo, primero usted digo—"

"English! I don't speak that shit, you do," Nettie yelled at her. Maria took a deep breath to calm down.

"First, you tell me we need the two dudes at the bar, and I let that go last night. Now you are telling me that we need that monster, too?" She pointed toward the door. "¡Ay, mi Dios!" Maria threw her hands in the air.

"Chill ya roll! Don't call him a monster. You don't even know him like that. He is an old friend and I don't have to stand here and explain shit to you. I've known him since we were kids, way before I met you. So kill all that noise you making." Nettie frowned at her.

Maria knew how far to push Nettie so she backed off a little.

"I'm saying, Netta, you don't tell me what's going on. I come home and see this man in our kitchen, and it scared me. You know I got your back, mamí, but you won't let me know what's going on." Maria sat on the bed.

"Look, Maria, this insecure bullshit is wearing me out. I don't have time to call you every time I need to make a move. You gonna have to trust me and that's it. I think you owe my boy an apology too." Nettie walked out of the bedroom, closing the door behind her.

That's the problem, Maria thought. She really didn't trust Nettie. She loved her, but didn't fully trust her. When Zola, Nettie's ex-lover, was alive, Nettie would spend a lot of time with Maria. She talked about Zola all the time, as if Maria didn't mean as much to her. Zola this and Zola that. But when Zola didn't have time for her, Nettie would come running back to Maria. Maria was always there for her, even through the times when Nettie was on her I'm-into-men-this-month kicks.

Nettie and Meat sat at the kitchen table while she explained to him what she needed. He listened intently without saying a word. He watched Nettie's lips move while she talked. They were soft-looking and full. Her lips were pink and matched her olive skin perfectly. It didn't matter what Nettie wanted him to do. He already knew he would do anything for her.

Maria finally came out of the bedroom when she heard laughter.

They had just finished discussing business and were now reminiscing. When Maria walked into the kitchen she tried to look at Meat, but couldn't stomach his looks. She looked down at her feet instead.

"I'm sorry for the way I acted. I thought you were robbing

the apartment," Maria said.

Meat nodded his head and smiled at Maria.

"It's all good, shorty. Me and Nette go way back."

Maria sat next to Nettie at the table and Nettie filled her in on her conversation with Meat.

CHAPTER 28

It had been a few weeks and the blocks were doing well for Nettie and her crew. The product was getting low and it would soon be time to re-up. But without a direct connect to cop from, that only meant one thing—they needed to hit Leroy again.

TJ and Tyler had become accustomed to their newfound occupations. Their popularity in school had risen considerably. TJ was laid back and reserved, whereas Tyler had dove headfirst into his elevated popularity status.

He had begun to cut classes in school and even had a couple girls checking for him. TJ tried to school Tyler that the kids that hung around him were groupies and not his real friends. He tried to show Tyler that when he didn't have money, he had no friends. Now that Tyler was gettin' money, everybody was sweating him. But Tyler, being as naïve as he was, and craving the attention he was now getting and couldn't see it.

The two of them were posted up in their usual spot on the block. TJ was kicking knowledge to Tyler once again. Tyler stood there, looking at TJ with the screw face.

"Yeah, I hear you talking, but you ain't hearing me, yo," Tyler said in his new hood lingo that came from nowhere. "But check it, the shorties is jockin' my dick and I'm gon' give it to them." He held his crotch.

TJ stood there, shaking his head. Just then Dice pulled up onto the block and TJ walked off to serve a customer.

"What up, money?" Tyler held his hand out for some dap.

"What's good, T-Y?" They shook hands and bumped shoulders.

"Yo, man, we low. When you gonna drop off some more work?" Tyler asked

"Soon, man, soon. Yo, how y'all doing out here?" Dice asked, leaning up against the building.

Dice lit up the blunt he had been holding in his hand.

"Aw, man, it's lovely. We got shit on lock out this bitch!"

Dice chuckled as he pulled deeply on the lit blunt. He then offered it to Tyler. Tyler gladly grabbed the blunt and commenced to smoking.

TJ walked up and shook Dice's hand.

"Yo, man, what you doing?" he asked Tyler, noticing he was smoking.

"What it look like?" Tyler asked while holding in the smoke, which made his voice sound funny.

"When you start smoking?" TJ asked, not believing his eyes.

"Man, I *been* blazin'," Tyler said, passing the blunt back to Dice.

"You want to hit this?" Dice asked TJ.

"Naw, I'm good." TJ walked away, seeing another customer approaching.

"Yo, Dice man, when you gonna hit me off with a gat?"

"What?" Dice laughed. It was funny to him how just a few weeks ago Tyler was this corny dweeb standing in front of TJ's house and now, suddenly, he was this thug.

"A gun, nigga. I need to be holdin', standing out here on these streets. In case a nigga wanna pop off, I'ma have to make it rain!" he bragged loudly. Dice continued to laugh.

"Yo, you a funny dude, man. I'll see what I can do. In the meantime, finish up the package and hit me." Dice gave Tyler what was left of the blunt and got in his car.

TJ walked back over to Tyler.

"Yo, man, what's up wit' you?" TJ asked.

"What you tryna' say, man?" Tyler responded.

"You out here, wildin' out, smoking blunts and talkin' loud."

"Listen, man, I'm being me. This who I am," Tyler said, tossing the roach to the ground.

"A-Yo, for real? You headed for the gutter, man. You only been out here like three weeks, and all of a sudden you actin' like you hard and shit. Tyler, man, I'm telling you, slow ya roll," TJ said seriously.

"Man, stop bendin' my ear back. Let's just get money! You beatin' me over the head with the bullshit. You need to be worried about this paper we tryna get and fuck all that other shit." Tyler walked off to serve a customer.

"A'ight, so y'all know what to do, right?" Nettie asked the ladies.

They all nodded their heads and stood.

"Have y'all heard anything about the robbery we did circulating at the club?" Nettie asked them.

"I heard that dude Stacks got blamed for it and they found him dead," Yuming answered.

"That's what's up." Nettie shook her head.

"You're not coming on this test run?" Yuming asked Nettie.

"Naw, Yuming, I'm gonna sit this one out. I got other business to take care of and I can't be in two places at once. But, trust, I will be there when we actually do the job. Maria, you know what's up, so make sure y'all get it down pat because I don't want no fuck-ups when it's time to do the hit. Stick to the script, Shawnee," Nettie said.

"Shawnee? Why you putting me on blast?" Shawnee asked, offended.

"Bitch, ain't nobody putting you on blast. I'm saying, I know you, so I'm just making sure you understand that Maria is running this here in my absence."

Nettie was sending the women, Meat, Dice and Click on a trial run of the job they were going to pull off next. Nate, Dice, and Click had done the run for Leroy, so the information Nate held—along with Nettie's strategy—made for a perfect hit. Since this job was different from the other one, she wanted to make sure that everyone was comfortable with it.

"I heard you the first four times you said it." Shawnee rolled her eyes at Nettie.

"I like it when you get feisty with me, Shawnee. Keep it up and I'm gonna have to show you how I tame wild bitches like you." Nettie looked at her with seduction in her eyes.

"Oh, hell-to-the-no!" Shawnee got up from the chair and headed toward the door.

Nettie and the rest of the ladies burst into laughter. Nettie then walked over to Maria and went to kiss her on the lips, but Maria turned her cheek. Nettie looked at her strangely. Maria never looked Nettie in the eyes. It was as if she was avoiding eye contact with Nettie.

"I'll call you, Netta, when I get back home," Maria said, leaving the apartment to catch up with the others.

Nettie stood there, staring at the closed door for a few more seconds and then she went to get dressed for her meeting with Wild.

CHAPTER 29

It was midnight when Detective Daniels pulled up in front of Janet's house. He put the truck in park and looked over at her. She was already looking at him and smiling while she held the doggy-bag from the restaurant in her lap.

"Thank you for taking time out of your busy schedule to feed me. Even though you stood me up the night you were supposed to take me to the diner," she said sarcastically in a playful manner. He smiled at her.

"You're welcome. It was the least I could do, and let the record show I didn't stand you up. I called you and told you I couldn't make it."

"So when am I gonna see you again?" she asked him.

"I don't know, Janet. I'll call you."

Janet sat there, looking straight ahead. Just then she thought she saw her son, Tyler and TJ, walking up the street. She squinted her eyes, trying to focus. Once they got closer, she realized it was him. Detective Daniels followed her eyes and spotted the young boys bopping up the street toward them.

"You know them?" Detective Daniels asked, not recognizing Tyler at first. But he recognized TJ to be the young boy he saw at the murder scene.

Detective Daniels had only seen Janet's children from the inside of his patrol truck. He had never had the pleasure of meeting them. Janet wanted it that way. She didn't want to bring a bunch of men around her children unless she knew for sure the man she was seeing was going to be there for the duration.

From what Detective Daniels could see of the boys walking up the street, if one of them was Tyler, he was not the nerdy boy he had seen standing on the porch prior to this night. What he was looking at were two young boys who dressed the part of a hustlers. The very kind of street garbage he was trying to clean up. Detective Daniels didn't want to judge a book by its cover, for the simple fact that lots of the kids these days dressed the part, but were not actually playing the game. But Tyler did look like he was playing the game.

TJ went into the front door of his house while Tyler walked around to the back of the house, clearly sneaking in. Janet looked at her watch and rolled her eyes. It was after midnight on a school night and he was trying to sneak in.

"Is that your son, Janet?" Detective Daniels asked, puzzled.

"Yeah, that was him. Let me go so I can find out where he is coming from and why he is even out of the house."

"I barely recognized him, Janet."

She looked away from him and out the window.

"Is everything all right?" he asked.

"I don't know, Rick. But I'm about to find out tonight. All I know is that lately I've noticed a change in him. He asked me for money to buy new clothes for school, but the clothes he's been wearing had to have cost more than the amount of money I gave him." She shook her head.

"So, let me ask you this, Janet. Do you think that your son is involved in drug trafficking?"

Janet whipped her head around and faced him.

"What are you trying to say, Rick? I can't believe you even said that." She was offended.

"No, baby, don't take it that way. I'm just saying, from the conversations I've had with you, I know your son is not that type of kid. But what I've seen tonight may suggest that he is into something," he said sincerely.

"It's police work with you all the time, ain't it, Rick? This is my son, not some thug you're chasing or case you're working. Stay outta my family business and chase those criminals out there in the streets, 'cause my son is not a criminal!" She got out of the truck, slamming the door behind her.

Once inside, she marched right to Tyler's room. He'd gotten in the bed and appeared to be asleep. Janet turned on the light, slamming his room door behind her. Tyler sat straight up in the bed.

"What's wrong, Ma?" he asked, sounding like the old Tyler.

"What's wrong? I'll tell you. Why did I just witness my son sneaking in the house after twelve o'clock in the morning, on a school night?" She stood there with her hands on her hips.

"What are you talking about, Ma?"

"Boy, don't make me go upside your head. Where were you?" Janet walked toward Tyler.

From the look on her face, he knew she was serious. He

swung his feet over the side of the bed, placing them on the floor.

"I-I was just . . . um . . ."

"Yeah, get ya lie together because if it ain't a good lie, you gonna be picking yourself up off of the floor. Now try me if you want," she warned him.

Tyler sat there, wracking his brain to come up with something to tell his mother. He knew that if she knew what he was really doing, then all hell was going to break loose.

WHACK!

She smacked him on the side of his head. Tyler was in shock as he looked up at his mother. It had been years since he'd been disciplined in that manner.

"Ma, chill out. You ain't give me a chance to explain," he said.

"Chill out? Boy, let me tell you something. I don't know what you're into, but you better make a U-turn and get out of it right now. When you think I don't know, Tyler, I know. You see your Uncle James? Your uncle ended up like that from those streets. I don't want that for you and your sister. I don't want y'all to struggle and live the life we grew up living. Tyler, you have choices in life and you have an opportunity to travel the right road. I know what you see out there in the streets, but trust me, that life does not have an insurance policy or a retirement plan. There are only two ways out son, and that's death or jail, and I don't want either one of those for you. What about you, Tyler? Do you want that?" she asked as tears ran down her face.

Tyler sat with his head held low. He couldn't look at his mother cry. She had always worked hard to give him and his sister all that they needed. Even when she went away, she made sure that someone came by and checked on them. But it wasn't enough. He was tired of wearing outdated clothes. He was tired of being picked on because he was smart and unpopular and because he wasn't up on the latest of anything. He was tired of not being able to leave the block and sometimes the porch, because his mother was strict. He wanted to make his own way and do his own thing. Getting his own money made him feel superior and responsible.

"I hear you, Ma," he said, looking down at the floor.

Janet put her hand under his chin and lifted his head so that his eyes could meet hers.

"Do you really, Tyler?"

"Yeah, Ma."

"I know what I'm talking about, Tyler. Please trust me. There are some things in my past that you don't know about. Maybe one day I will sit down and tell you about it, but for now, trust me, son."

"I hear you, Ma."

"You're growing into a man and I know the little fast girls are out there chasing you." She smiled. "You are a handsome guy and I can see the peach fuzz coming in on your lip." She laughed.

Tyler smiled and moved his chin from her hand.

"Tyler, if at anytime you need to talk about *anything*, son, please come to me. Don't go to none of them negroes in the streets. Do you hear me?"

"Yeah, Ma, I hear you."

"All right, you get to sleep. You got school in the morning." Janet patted him on the shoulder.

Tyler lay back in the bed, looking up at the ceiling. What did his mother mean about some things she did in her past?

CHAPTER 30

Nettie pulled up to the corner and put the car in park. She then looked over at James.

"So you do understand that I need you to be on time, James?"

"Yeah, I got you, Nettie. I'm ya brother and I ain't gonna let you down. I appreciate you letting me get a piece of what you got going on."

"James, please. This is serious and I don't need you fucking this up, nor do I need you running ya mouth." She looked at him seriously.

"Baby sis," he looked at her sideways, "I'm ya big brother. I wouldn't do you like that," he assured her.

"Do you need me to pick you up or can you get there—never mind. I'll come through after eleven in two days," she told him. "I'll pick you up from right here."

"Okay," he said and then looked over at her with those almond-shaped eyes of his. "Can you let me hold something for now? You can take it outta my pay."

"You killing me, Jay," she said, irritated by his begging.

She gave him twenty dollars that she retrieved from her purse. He thanked her and got out of the vehicle.

-⟨⟩-⟨⟩-⟨⟩

Meanwhile . . .

Meat and Maria were sitting in the living room, engaged in a good conversation about how they had a lot in common. Meat loved to watch old western movies and Maria also liked to watch them. They both enjoyed watching the animal channel and professional wrestling. They sat and talked about previous matches and special events.

Meat came over because Nettie told him to meet her there after the trial run. She was already a half hour late. But it was okay with Maria because she was really starting to enjoy being in Meat's presence. She had come to overlook Meat's skin condition and he was turning out to be a really good-hearted guy. He made her laugh and he was smart. He told her how he and Nettie were neighbors when they were both young. Meat didn't tell Maria how he really felt about Nettie, since being in Maria's presence on several occasions he was starting to fall for her. It was easy for Meat to fall for any woman who gave him attention, even if the attention was strictly platonic. Meat took it to heart. He had a rough time trying to get into relationships because of his skin. He had played with the idea of having the keloids removed, to only be reminded by the physician that it would heal the same way, if not worse.

"Meat, what happened to your skin?" Maria asked him.

Meat looked at her and held his head low.

"I'm sorry. I shouldn't have asked," she said, touching his leg.

"It's okay. I will tell you."

Meat told Maria how he received the keloid scars. After listening to Meat's story, Maria came to admire him more. He hadn't let that crutch hold him back.

"Why don't you have it removed?"

"Can't. I've talked to different doctors about it. There's a chance of it healing the same way." Meat also told Maria how his body's healing process just stops and it doesn't repair the skin properly.

"Well, is there something you can take for it?"

"The doctors injected cortisone steroid drugs when I was younger, but that didn't work either."

"Oh," she said, fiddling with her fingers.

"Hey," he said, lifting her chin so that their eyes met. "I'm good with the way I look. Don't worry about me. I've looked like this for a long time."

They sat gazing into each other's eyes.

Nettie looked at her watch. It was twelve-forty-five p.m. She was supposed to have met Meat at the house hours ago. Maria didn't call her on her cell, so she thought he might not have gotten there yet. Wild sat on the passenger's side of her car while they were watching Leroy's house. Nettie and Wild had become quite the team. They had talked about many things and joining forces to get rid of Leroy was one of them. Unbeknownst to the others, Wild and Nettie began to brainstorm the perfect plan to rob and kill Leroy. Tonight was the beginning of the end for Leroy Jenkins. Wild explained everything to Nettie. He told her about Leroy's routine and his security. Nate had played a big part in giving

Wild that information.

Trust was not something that Wild usually had for anyone. But after spending time getting to know Nettie and seeing how down she was, he was wide open with trust for her. She seemed to trust him, too, or so he thought.

They sat and watched Leroy's mansion and pointed out key points on the preparation of the hit. They also discussed who would play what role, and who would execute what part of the plan. Wild and Nettie had decided that they wouldn't tell the rest of the crew who they were hitting. That way no one would make any mistakes out of fear of Leroy. They had already planned to take the biggest of the profit and split it between the two of them since they were the masterminds behind the plan.

As Wild talked, Nettie looked at him. His handsome features were a turn-on to her. They were hard but sexy. She knew he was a dominant man and would love to have him lying between her thighs. She envisioned him with a hump in his back, dicking her down hard. Although she strapped on and was the aggressor when she was with a woman, she was definitely the woman when she had sex with men. She liked it rough and hard.

Wild brought her out of her trance when he rubbed the side of her face with the back of his hand.

"You a'ight?" he asked.

"Oh, yeah. I'm so good right now." She smiled.

"Looks like you was in another place and time."

"Yeah, something like that." She looked away.

He turned her face toward his and went in for a kiss, but then he suddenly stopped.

"What's wrong?" she asked.

"Nate told me about how you carry a blade in ya mouth. I'm not tryna lose my tongue." He smiled at her.

"Oh, so Nate doing it like that, huh? What else did Nate tell you about me?"

"Hey, keep me outta that," Wild said, surrendering.

"Wild, listen. If there is anything you want to know about me, just ask. The blade is gone, Wild. Ever since shooting a gun, I felt a rush like no other. See . . ." She opened her mouth, moving her tongue around to show that there was no blade.

Wild nodded his head as he stared into her eyes. He leaned in to kiss her again. They kissed slow and passionately. She felt for his rod, not wasting time and began to massage it. It began to grow in length and width. Wild kissed her neck and whispered into her ear.

"Let's go back to your place."

She knew she could never bring him back to Maria's place. That was all she needed, to hear Maria's mouth about how she was fucking men in the house where they slept.

"Naw, let's get a room."

"I'm wit' that," he said, looking into her eyes.

Nettie's twat was hot. She was on fire and couldn't wait to get a piece of Wild. She knew she would have to hear Maria's mouth about how she kept them waiting and how disrespectful she was. But little did Nettie know that Meat was waist deep inside Maria in the very bed that she and Nettie slept in.

CHAPTER 31

Two days later

Meat drove the black GMC Yukon with all five of the ladies in it. Maria sat up front on the passenger's side. Maria and Meat stole a few glances at each other every now and then, sending their vibes at each other. Everyone rode in silence.

Meat pulled the truck to the corner and killed the engine. They were three blocks away from another one of Leroy's main stash houses, located in the Dodd Town section of East Orange.

Nate had become closer to Leroy than when he first came on board. Since they now did the pickup and delivery for Leroy, they had actually delivered the huge shipment to the spot they were getting ready to rob.

Nate talked to Nettie and Wild about not delivering the shipment, since he would be driving with it on the back of the rental truck he drove. But Wild insisted that he stick to the script and deliver Leroy's product to the destination assigned.

Nettie did a mike-and-ear plug check on everyone's system from the spot where she, Wild and Nate had been sitting.

"Panther One, mike check," she said into the pin on her coat.

"Panther One, roger," Maria said into her pin.

"Panther Two, mike check."

"Panther Two, roger," Yuming said into her pin.

Nettie did this to all the women and then to Meat, Dice, and Click. The mikes and earpieces were functioning properly.

"A'ight, let's see how this pans out," Nettie said to no one in particular.

Nettie, Wild and Nate sat in a Ford F150 parked at the top of the hill. They all had binoculars and were watching the scene.

Dice and Click were on standby in the U-Haul truck, waiting for the signal to go in as back-up muscle for the women.

The ladies exited the truck, all wearing their black cat suits and black leather jackets. They all carried black duffel bags thrown over their shoulders.

Yuming moved through the night just like a panther. She was quick and light on her feet. The others went separate ways. The house was surrounded by thirty acres of woods. Yuming ran through the wooded area located next to the mini-mansion-style home. There was a barbwire fence that went around the entire house. The house had four security cameras located at each outer corner in trees. On the grounds were four security guards and they walked the grounds in their designated areas at each corner of the house. There were two Rottweiler's chained to the fence at the front entrance of the home. Outside the gates, at that front entrance, there was a small security booth with an armed guard.

Nate explained the setup inside the house and had drawn the best floor plan he could from what he remembered when he dropped off the birds during the delivery shipment. Nate managed to see the whole ground floor in its entirety. He was only able to see three rooms upstairs, though. He knew the shipment was in the basement, because that's where they had carried the product when they unloaded it from the truck.

Meat sat patiently in the driver's seat. He began to think about Maria and how she was such a good woman. He found himself really falling for her and he knew she was falling for him as well. He watched through his binoculars as she sat just yards away with the others, waiting for the go-ahead from Yuming.

Yuming had finally made it to her destination. She sat in the bushes just a few feet from the fence. She could see a guard leaning against a tree on the grounds. He was talking on his cell phone and holding his MAC-10 with one hand. This was perfect for her, as he was distracted by the phone conversation and she would be able to take care of him with no problem. It often made Yuming laugh at how most Americans weren't disciplined. Any little thing was a distraction to them.

She went into her bag and pulled out her mask. She pulled it down tight over her head and ponytail. She retrieved a throwing star from her bag of knives. She then grabbed her nun chucks from the bag, shoving them under the belt she had around her waist. She zipped up the bag and threw it over her shoulder so the straps came down across her chest. She placed the four short, sharp knives in her belt, two on each side. She then placed the throwing star in her mouth and crawled like a snake through the bushes.

Yuming reached the fence behind the house and sat still, like a cat ready to pounce on its prey. She then reached down the side of her boot, pulled out some wire cutters and began carefully cutting the fence from the bottom while never taking her cat-like eyes off the armed security guard. He seemed to be really enjoying his conversation on the phone instead of patrolling the grounds as he was instructed.

Yuming was finally able to cut a circle large enough for her slim frame to fit through. She removed the duffel bag and shoved it through the fence. She then slithered through the hole in the fence.

Once on the other side of the fence, Yuming lay flat on her stomach and inched her way toward the guard, whose back was facing her. Once she was close enough, she took the star out of her mouth and threw it like a Frisbee. It whizzed through the air like a bullet, finally finding its resting spot in the back of the guard's head.

Yuming rolled onto her back, lying perfectly still, blending into the night. She was waiting to see any reaction from inside the house. When nothing happened, she knew that security inside the house was not watching the cameras.

She grabbed her duffel bag from where she left it by the fence and threw it back over her shoulder. She ran low to the ground over to the security guard that lay on the ground.

She felt for his pulse and there wasn't one. She then began to drag him back over by the fence. He wasn't a large man, but his dead weight was enough to cause her to perspire. Once she reached the fence, she spoke into her pin.

"Panther Two to Eagle One, you got your eyes on?"

"Eagle One, yeah, it's all clear," Nate said as he looked through the binoculars.

"Let's stay focused, people," Nettie announced into everyone's earpiece.

Yuming then spoke into the pin again.

"Panther Two to Road Dog One."

"Road Dog One," Dice answered.

"Positioned and ready," Yuming said.

Yuming sat there for several seconds until Dice showed up at the fence. He squeezed through the fence, getting caught on the cut wire several times.

"Damn, girl, you couldn't cut that hole no bigger than that? You got me scraping my shit all up," he complained, rubbing his leg.

Yuming simply looked at him before she took off into the darkness, running low to the ground.

Dice began to strip the guard of his clothing and put it on himself. Once he got dressed, he noticed that the guard's clothes were big on him, but he made a few adjustments and managed to make it fit well. Dice pulled the black fitted cap down onto his head to conceal as much of his face as possible. He picked up the MAC-10 and walked back over to the tree, holding the guard's walkie-talkie in his hand.

"Road Dog One to Panther Three and Four," Dice said into the ring on his finger.

Both women answered simultaneously.

"All clear," he said.

One minute later the Hispanic sisters came through the opening in the fence. Dice kept a watchful eye while Jasmine scaled a nearby tree like cat. Once up the tree, she spray-painted the camera lenses black. She then shimmied down the tree and she and Marisa took off running toward the house. In the meantime, Yuming had killed another guard by throwing her mini-knife, hitting him on the side of the neck. She had dragged him to the fence and cut the wire there, too. She then contacted Click, who killed another guard and took his clothes as well. Click then contacted Shawnee and Maria. They followed the exact same procedure by spraying the camera's lenses. Now, with everyone in place, it was show time.

CHAPTER 32

Detective Daniels sat in his truck and waited. The back door opened and his informant got into the backseat.

"What's up, man?" the informant asked.

"You tell me," Detective Daniels said.

"Well, I'm not sure just yet, but I might have something big for you. I'm just waiting to get some more information on it."

"Okay, so what are you talking about?"

"About a lot of drugs," the informant said.

"Yeah? Where and when?"

"That's what I'm waiting for. It should be tonight or maybe tomorrow."

"Okay, so when you find out, let me know. Have you heard anything on the murders on the street?"

"Naw, nothing yet."

Detective Daniels reached into his pocket and pulled out a twenty. He passed it over the seat to the informant, who grabbed the money and got out of the truck.

Detective Daniels sat there, looking in his notebook at the notes he had been taking the last several weeks. He was no closer to finding the culprit of the double murders of the two young teens than he had been. He looked at the notes he wrote in reference to the new evidence found on the murder of Beverly Downing at the cemetery several months ago. A partial finger print was discovered and he was waiting for the results to come back. It wasn't the cleanest print, but with technology today, he knew it would be eventually matched.

TJ and Tyler sat in the basement of Tyler's house counting the money they had made. They were out of work and had been waiting, like Dice instructed, until he brought more.

"Yo, man, they need to stop bullshitting and bring some more product. My grip ain't looking right," Tyler stated.

"That's 'cause you out here wild'n out thinking you a baller. You need to save your money, man," TJ said.

Suddenly they could hear talking through the vents. It sounded like a male's voice speaking to Janet. Although the sounds were muffled, they could still make out the words.

"So do you know where the baby came from?" the male asked.

"No, I don't. All I know is Nettie showed up here one day with the boy. She said it was hers and she got burned out of her apartment and needed a place for the baby to stay until she got on her feet," Janet answered.

"Well, you and I both know that is not Nettie's baby."

"Tell me about it," Janet said.

"Okay. So do you have any clue whose baby this is and what she's doing with it?" he asked.

"I really don't know. Do you have any idea?"

"I got a feeling on something, but I can't prove it. Will you help me?"

"Sure, anything to get this baby to his rightful parents. I swear, I don't know what's gotten into her," Janet said, looking away.

"Well, we about to find out."

"So what made you come by here and talk to me?"

"I have my reasons," he said.

"Like what, for example?"

"What do you mean?" he asked.

"What made you think that this baby was not Nettie's? I mean, I know it's not hers, but my mother is soft on her, so there wasn't much I could do. After thinking about it, I felt that we couldn't put a baby out in the streets, no matter whose he was. I wouldn't want anyone to turn their backs on my kids. Now, tell me what makes you think it's not hers?"

"Well, for one, the baby looks nothing like her."

"He could look like the father. What else?" Janet asked.

"He does look like someone I knew and plus, the baby got green eyes."

"Okay, yes, the baby does have green eyes. So what?"

"Well, I knew one person that lived in the city of Newark that had green eyes but she's dead."

"Do you think it's her baby?"

"Well, yeah, I do, because she had those same green eyes and . . . never mind. I just got a feeling. Are you going to help me or not?" he asked Janet.

"Sure. I said I would."

"Well, I'll keep in touch with you. Here's my cell number.

Call me when you find out anything and I'll let you know what I find out."

"Okay," she said.

Janet stood there after she closed the door behind him and thought for a moment. She went into her daughter's room where she shared a room with the baby. She walked over to the crib and stared at the baby as he slept peacefully. Her mind was racing with all kinds of thoughts, especially about this strange visit tonight. She walked out of the room to go to bed. She would figure this situation out later.

Leroy sat behind his desk at the pool hall. He was leaned back in his chair, receiving one hell of a blow job. At his age, he still had fire in him and he moaned as the chocolate beauty gave him a head job like no other. He wasn't a well-endowed man, so it was easy for her to deep-throat his manhood. As he reached his climax and busted off in her mouth, he made sure she swallowed before he allowed her to stand to her feet.

A knock came at the door and he put away his limp tool. He spun his chair around and told the chocolate beauty to open the door.

In walked Dak with Detective Daniels on his heels. The chocolate beauty didn't even wait to be told to leave. She closed the door behind her when she left.

"Detective, to what do I owe this pleasure?" Leroy asked.

"Why haven't you come down to the station like I asked?" Detective Daniels asked, sitting in the chair in front of the desk.

Leroy looked over at Dak and they both smiled. In fact, he and Dak did go to the station. But the detective was not there.

"I did, detective, but you weren't there."

"You can't bullshit a bullshitter, Leroy," Detective Daniels said.

"No bullshit, detective. Hey, isn't it past your bedtime?" Leroy joked, looking at his three-hundred-thousand-dollar watch. Detective Daniels didn't see the humor.

"The two kids that got murdered over there on Eighteenth and Isabella worked for you."

"What two kids?"

"Don't play games with me, Leroy. You know damn well who I'm talking about."

"Frankly, I don't know what you're talking about, Rick. I have a mass of employees that work for me. I have the supermarket, the Realtors, the gas station. I mean, hell, it could be anybody. So now tell me; what two kids?" Leroy looked at him seriously.

"The two kids that were pushing dope for you, you son of a bitch! Day-Day and Unique were their street names!" Detective Daniels was pissed.

In the detective's eyes, Leroy had no heart. How could a man put kids on the streets to feed poison to other kids? This really pissed off Detective Daniels.

Dak began to move closer to Leroy, ready to protect his boss. Leroy saw him moving out of the corner of his eyes and held up his hand to stop Dak. Detective Daniels looked over at Dak with piercing eyes.

"Go 'head, punk, make a move." He taunted Dak.

"Detective." Leroy interrupted the staring match between Dak and Detective Daniels. "Like I said to you, I have many employees working for me and those names don't sound familiar. However, I can have my people run a check on those names to see if they were actually employed at one of my businesses. Other than that, I don't do the drug business." Leroy put his elbows on the desk.

"You're gonna slip up, Leroy and when you do, I am going to be the muthafucka that catches you slipping." Detective Daniels stood and pointed in Leroy's face.

Dak charged at Detective Daniels, but stopped suddenly when Detective Daniels pulled out his gun and pointed it in his face.

"Yeah, big boy, bring it. You ain't so tough now, are you?" Detective Daniels asked as he began to back toward the door slowly. "You better get ya boy in check, Leroy. He don't know who he fucking with."

Leroy sat there, grinning at the detective as he watched him back his way to the door.

"Relax Dak, he's a pussy. Ain't no need in getting yourself worked up over this cocksucker."

"We'll see who'll be sucking cock when I put your old ass behind bars," Detective Daniels said as he opened the door and backed out of the office.

"What the fuck was that?" Dak asked Leroy once the detective was gone.

"I don't know, but I think he knows something. We gotta keep our noses clean, Dak. That muthafucka is starting to be a pain in my ass. He probably got my shit bugged." Leroy picked up the phone and checked it. "Dak, have somebody come in here tomorrow and sweep for bugs in this joint. I think I'm gonna take a little trip south and meet with Tony face to face. He owes me another favor and I'm going to cash in that favor."

"A'ight boss. You need me to escort you?"

"Naw, I need you here to make sure my shit is straight while I'm gone. I'll get a couple of the other guys to come with me. Maybe I'll call my man Nate and his boys."

CHAPTER 33

There were four security men inside the house and, as Yuming suspected, they weren't paying attention to the cameras. The men sat around a table and played cards, confident in the security guards that patrolled the grounds. The shipment was in the basement of the mansion, sitting on a pallet. The breakdown wasn't scheduled until noon the next day.

Meat walked up to the front gate acting as if he was drunk. He was dressed in torn jeans and a ripped overcoat. He sang as he approached the gate. The guard that sat in the mini-booth emerged to inspect the stranger. The dogs began to bark ferociously. They were going wild as their deep-sounding barks echoed through the night. The two front guards that patrolled the grounds came running to see what was wrong.

"Yo, man, hold it right there," the guard from the mini-booth said.

The other two guards reached the gate at that time and calmed the dogs by petting them, letting them know everything was all right.

"Heeeeyyy, I got sunshine, ooooonnn a clooouudy daaaay!" Meat sang an old song by the Temptations.

The dogs began to bark again.

"Yo, man, keep it moving. You can't come in here," the guard said.

"Whatchu mean, I can't be here? I live here, sucka," Meat drawled. He stood there, squinting his eyes, trying to focus as he swayed back and forth.

"What's up, man?" one of the guards from inside the gate asked the guard from the mini-booth.

"This leather face nigga drunk as hell and I'm tryna get him to keep it movin'."

"Yo, muthafucka, get the fuck off the property now!" the guard from inside the gate yelled.

"Yeah, nigga, bounce before I put a bullet in ya ass. With that nasty ass skin hanging off yo' face," the other guard from inside the gate co-signed.

"Hoooowww you muthafuckaaaas gone tell me I-I can't come to my own hooouse?" Meat struggled to talk.

Just then Meat dove to the ground. Before the three guards knew what hit them, Dice and Click were standing behind them holding the MAC-10s they'd lifted from the dead guards. They riddled bullets at the three guards, ripping flesh from their bodies as each bullet entered. They shot the dogs as well. Meat jumped to his feet and Dice opened the gate.

Maria and Shawnee were already at the other two cameras, spray-painting the lenses black.

Meat grabbed the dead guard, dragged him through the gate and tossed his body into the bushes like a sack of potatoes. Click was already pulling one of the other guards into the bushes as well. Dice began removing the dogs from view when he realized they were chained. He went through one of the dead guard's pockets until he found keys and began working the lock that held the thick chains together. In the meantime, Meat got rid of the third guard's body in the bushes. He picked up both guards' AK-47's, throwing the straps over his shoulders. Click closed the gate and they proceeded up the driveway toward the mansion.

The guards inside the house didn't hear the gunshots. They were high from smoking weed and drinking. They had the music blasting and continued to gamble without a clue about what was going on outside the house.

Everyone was in place and checked in with Nettie.

"Panther One to base," Maria said into her mike.

"Yeah, Panther One," Nettie responded.

"Panther One and Five in position."

"Panther Three to base," Jasmine said.

"Go 'head, Panther Three."

"Panther Three and Four in position,"

"Road Dog One to Base…" Dice said.

"Yeah, Road Dog One."

"Road Dog One, Two, and Three in position."

Nettie sat there, waiting for Yuming to tell her she was in position and ready. When there was no call, Nettie reached out to her.

"Base to Panther Two."

Still there was no response from Yuming and this was not like her. She was the most thorough of the bunch, including the guys. She was precise and on point; something wasn't right.

"Base to Panther Two," Nettie said a little louder.

Nate and Wild looked at each other. Wild pulled out his guns and checked the clips. Nate followed his lead and began to do the same.

"Shit!" Nettie said, reaching under the seat for her weapons. "Everyone, hold your positions!" She was getting pissed.

"Base to Road Dog Three," Nettie called out to Meat.

"Road Dog Three to base."

"Panther Two didn't respond to position check. Can you get over there and see what's going on?" Nettie asked Meat.

"Road Dog Three doing a spot check," Meat said as he started to make his way to Yuming's position.

Yuming heard the whole conversation but she couldn't respond. She was caught between a rock and a hard place. She was hiding underneath the back porch, watching one of the security men piss from the top steps down onto the ground. Urine ran from the cemented ground back down to where she was located under the porch. Steam rose from the warm liquid when it hit the cold cement.

Yuming could have easily eliminated the drunken guard, but that wasn't the plan. She had to wait for the go-ahead. As she lay there and urine ran past her head, she wanted to break the guard's neck with her bare hands. She was so vexed.

Finally the guard finished relieving himself and staggered back into the house. Just as Yuming slithered from under the porch, Meat crept around the corner.

"Yuming, what's up?" he whispered. "You didn't answer for ready check."

"You don't want to fuckin' know," she whispered back

clearly, showing anger. "Let's do this shit so I can go home and take a bath. Panther Two to base, ready."

Nettie was relieved to know all was still on point. She took a deep breath.

"A'ight, hold ya positions. Go on my word."

Wild started the truck and drove it closer. The threesome got out of the truck and began the walk through the woods toward the mansion.

Once Nate, Nettie and Wild got to a certain part in the woods where they could see the entire house, they spread out and began to look through their binoculars. They looked into the windows of the house, trying to locate bodies on each floor. From what they could each detect, there was no movement on the second and third floors.

"Base to any Road Dogs," Nettie said into the pin mike.

"Road Dog One, go 'head base," Dice said.

"Check the windows for movement near the front door."

"It's done, base," Dice said, having already checked. He was anxiously waiting for the go-ahead signal.

"Road Dogs execute to the front door," Nettie said.

Click pulled out a set of lock picks and started working on the front door when Wild interrupted.

"Base to Road Dogs," he said.

"Road Dog one to base, what's up?" Dice asked.

"Cease front door execution!"

Click pulled the picks out of the lock and looked up at Dice.

"Road Dog Two to base, what's up?" Click asked, irritated. He was sick of all the talk and just wanted to kick in the front door and go in blazing. As far as he was concerned, to hell with all the formalities.

"What's up? Why you stop him, Wild?" Nettie walked up on the back of him.

"There's an alarm system on the house." He pointed to a small box located in the top corner of the arch over the front door. He was looking through his binoculars and instructed Nettie to look. She looked at the front door and saw it too. Obviously the team failed to notice it on the trial run.

"So, that doesn't mean the alarm is on."

"Well I don't want to take that chance," Wild responded.

"Well what we gonna do?" she asked.

"We gonna get them to come outside of the house." He walked off toward the house and Nettie followed behind him.

"Road Dogs, change of plan. Use the walkie-talkies you lifted from the stiffs and call a raid. Bang on the front door, bust out one of the windows and take cover. This will get them to run to the front, but believe me, they gonna come out blazin'," Wild said.

"Wait! Hold ya positions!" Nettie instructed them. "Wild, do you think that's a good idea? Its gonna 'cause all types of noise and someone may hear it." Wild looked at her sideways.

"Nettie, there isn't another house for at least a half mile. Besides you didn't think about that when they let off on the guards out front."

Nate came running up to them.

"Yo, what's up? We way out here in west bumble fuck and y'all niggas want to hold a conversation. We're wasting a lot of time. Let's do this shit and be out!"

"Fuck it!" Nettie said. "Bust them doors down and go in

buckin'! Now!" she said as Wild and Nate took off running toward the house.

Dice and Click stod back and counted to three. They both ran and kicked in the front door. The alarm sounded and the guards all scrambled from the table, grabbing their weapons and heading for the front of the house. Meat kicked in the backdoor and it flew off like paper. He pressed the trigger on the MAC-10, sending bullets flying. Click and Dice came in the front door, letting off before they even had a target to shoot.

The two guards bringing up the rear were hit in the back several times by the bullets coming from Meat. The first two guards dove to the floor and took cover behind furniture.

Yuming stayed outside and took cover underneath the outside window shield. The other ladies had hit the dirt outside from their positions, trying to avoid stray bullets. Dice and Click took cover in the house in the adjacent room. One guard fired at Meat, who was standing by the counter in the kitchen doorway. The other guard kept his attention on the room Dice and Click were in. Wild reached the house first, with Nate not too far behind. He could see Click and Dice in the other room. Dice was hit in the leg and he was sitting on the floor, holding it.

"How many we talking, Click?" Wild asked.

"I think it's only two. Dice is hit."

"I know. I can see that." They spoke to each other threw their rings.

Nate had peeped in the window when bullets came flying through, shattering the glass. He ducked just in time to avoid getting killed. He lay on the ground with glass all over him and several cuts on his face.

"You a'ight?" Wild asked.

"I'm good," Nate said, brushing glass off.

Wild ran into the house toward the guards and dove onto the floor, doing a forward roll. He came out of the roll spraying with two guns in his hands, while ducking bullets from the guard's guns.

Both guards were now dead. Click, Meat and Nate stood there looking at Wild like he was a superhero. They had never seen anything like that except on television.

"Damn, nigga, what? You got super powers or some shit?" Click asked.

"Man, fuck the bullshit. Get them ladies in there to lift this shit and let's be out. Nate, you go get the U-Haul and Click, check the rest of the house. Meat, go with the ladies and get the shit from the basement."

Nettie walked in the front door and stood there, looking around. She saw Dice trying to stand up and went over to help him.

"We gonna have to get him to a hospital," she said.

"Naw, we can't do that. I'll take care of him after we get outta here. Take him back to the truck and wait," Wild instructed.

Nettie looked at him with lust in her eyes. He was so sexy to her, the way he took control of the situation.

It took them fifteen minutes to pack the product and check the rest of the house. They got lucky and found five hundred thousand dollars in the house as well.

Five minutes later they were on their way back to Maria's crib.

CHAPTER 34

Back at Maria's house, everyone was complaining about what went wrong during the hit.

"What the hell happened back there?" Shawnee asked.

"Yeah," a couple of them said in unison.

"I don't know, but all I know is that shit was whack. I say, fuck all that technical shit! That's how we should have went in from the rip!" Click said, wired up from the alcohol he had consumed.

"Whose idea was that anyway?" Dice asked, feeling no pain.

Dice drank half of a fifth of Crown Royal in order to numb his body from the pain of the bullet wound. He was stretched out on a blanket Nettie had put on the floor for him and Wild was carefully working on his leg. The bullet had only grazed his leg. The wound was deep enough that it required stitches and Wild was stitching him up.

"It was my plan. Why?" Nettie looked at Dice with evil eyes.

"I'm just saying, sis, the shit wasn't cool." He reached for the blunt Nate was passing him. "Ah! Damn, muthafucka, ease up!" he said to Wild.

"Yo, Wild, man, how you know how to do that?" Click asked.

"Let's just say I had to learn from personal experience in the past," Wild said, not looking up at Click.

"I mean, he got a kit and the whole nine." Click was amazed at the skills Wild had in stitching up the wound.

Wild did have personal experience with taking care of a gunshot wound. He was taught by an old friend with whom he did some time. In the business Wild was in, at times he did get shot at, and on occasion he was actually hit. Going to the hospital was not a option. It is the hospitals responsibility to report all gunshot wounds to the police. Going back to jail was out of the question for Wild, so he had to tend to his own wounds and he became quite good at it.

"Nettie, I thought it was a good plan. It worked for us when we did it alone the last time," Marisa interjected.

"Yeah, and it was just us ladies," Jasmine added.

"So what you saying, ma? 'Cause we was there, it got fucked up?" Nate asked her.

"No, papí. I'm saying it worked when we did it before. ¿Comprende?" Jasmine looked at him.

Nate blew her a kiss and she stuck up her middle finger. Nate laughed and drank from his glass of Hennessy.

"That was my bad. I should have told y'all to look for the alarm system." Wild came to Nettie's defense.

"Wild, you ain't got to explain shit to these muthafuckas. Anybody who don't like how we rollin' can bounce, 'cause y'all can get served just like them guards did tonight!" Nettie was offended by their badgering of her plan.

"Hold up, Nett. On the humble, I respect ya game ma, we just talking about what happened," Click said.

"Yeah, Netta, calm down," Maria said to her.

Nettie shot Maria a look. She was still heated with Maria from the way she acted before, so anything Maria said right now wouldn't be wise.

Maria saw the look and turned away. Meat caught the look and he didn't like it.

"Everybody just calm down for a minute." Meat stood with his body towered over the room. "We had some technical difficulties on this job, but we pulled it off as a team. We got the 'W', so let's not let a minor error turn us against each other."

"Yeah, it's easy for you to say: You ain't get shot, nigga," Dice said as Wild wiped his leg. "Yo, blaze up, Nate. Let's just get faded," he said as Wild helped him to the chair.

Everyone sat in silence and Meat went to sit next to Maria. She gazed into his eyes, telling him thank you. Nettie saw the interaction and went into the kitchen.

Wild followed her into the kitchen while the rest of the crew continued to talk about what had happened.

"What's wrong, baby?" Wild asked Nettie.

"Nothing. I'm good." She stood there, looking pissed.

"Naw, don't lie. Listen, it all worked out and we got the shit. I got a place we can store it 'cause you can't keep it all here," Wild said.

"Good looking, but I got a spot already set up to put it."

"You sure? Because my man, who is our best customer, he got a big basement and a crew that can unload it quick."

"Hmm, naw, I got something set up. Plus my brother is

waiting for me to come through."

"Your brother? I didn't know you had a brother," Wild said, surprised.

"Yeah. I got a sister, too. You'll meet him when we get there."

Nate walked into the kitchen. "So what's up? What we gonna do? Stock?" Nate asked.

"I want you to take Dice home. Me and Nate gonna go take the weight to the spot I was telling you about."

"The spot ya brother told you about?" Nate looked at her sideways.

"Yeah, why? What's wrong?" she asked.

Wild stood there, looking at them back and forth, like he was watching a tennis match.

"Come on, Nett. You sure ya brother is trustworthy?"

"I trust my brother, Nate. He ain't gonna trip like that with me, trust." She was confident.

"A'ight. It's on you, sis." Nate left the kitchen

Wild washed his hands in the sink and wiped them on a towel he had draped across his shoulder. He walked over to Nettie, leaned down and kissed her softly on the lips.

"So, what's up with ya brother?"

"He cool." Nettie avoided telling him the full truth.

"I'll tell you what: Why don't you take Dice home. Me, Nate and Click will handle the load?"

"I don't know, Wild. My brother is looking for me to come."

"You said Nate knows ya brother. Does ya brother know who Nate is?"

"Yeah," she said.

"Well then, Nate can just tell him what's up and that you sent us. Cool?"

She nodded. Wild turned her face to his and kissed her again.

"You wanna go pick up where we left off?" he whispered in her ear. A smile came across Nettie's face.

"Sure. I'll be at the hotel in our same room. I'll see you after y'all finish. Let's go split this money with them, so we can bounce." She walked back into the living room.

"Yo, anybody seen Cash?" Click asked.

Everybody shook their heads.

"I called him twice, but he never answered," Nettie said. "I guess he still feeling some kind of way because I put y'all on before he had a chance to tell y'all."

"That nigga is a punk!" Click said as he began to cough from the weed smoke.

"I think Cash might be a problem for us," Nate said.

"Well, if he a problem, then he gotta go," Wild said matter-of-factly.

"Cash? Naw, he ain't no problem. He just young, that's all," Nettie added.

"Naw, Nette. He's been acting funny," Click said.

"Cash is cool. Leave him alone. He got a little brother and sister to take care of. Who knows why he couldn't make it? Trust me, Cash is a good dude. Y'all always fuckin' with him. Just leave him alone," Nettie said as she grabbed the duffel bag with the money in it.

CHAPTER 35

After the money was split between the eleven of them, it came out to a little over forty-five thousand each. Wild, Nate and Click went out to take the shipment to the spot Nettie had set up. Nettie drove her car to take Dice home and told Meat to escort the ladies home. But Meat stayed behind with Maria and the other four ladies went their separate ways.

Wild and Nate rode in the U-Haul while Click drove Nate's car, following behind them.

"OK, make a left right here," Nate said.

"So, what's up with Nettie's brother?" Wild asked.

"He a fiend, man. He's been out there on that shit since as long as I can remember. They call him Black Santa."

"Word? So why would Nettie trust her brother to watch a shitload of coke and dope? That's like letting mice loose in a cheese factory." Wild looked over at Nate.

"True that. I feel you but you don't know Nettie like I do. If she wants it like this, then that's what it is."

Wild drove with a smirk on his face. From what he'd seen, Nettie was a woman through and through. He knew she was down for the crime, but he couldn't see her ever living up to the rumors that circulated about her. Wild knew a sinister bitch when he saw one and Nettie wasn't that bitch, at least not in his mind.

"Yeah, well, I pretty much know enough about Nettie to know that she trusts my judgment. You know me well enough to know I run me. Don't nobody else run me. There's gonna be a change in plans." Wild looked over at Nate.

"Yo, that's on you, man. I'm riding with you." Nate turned to look out the window.

Nettie helped Dice up the stairs and into his apartment that he shared with Click. After he got inside, she turned and left. Dice hopped over to the sofa and plopped down. Not even a good five minutes went by before someone rang the bell.

"Shit," he said, not wanting to get up off the sofa.

He hopped over to the window and opened it. The winter wind invaded the apartment. He lifted the screen and stuck his head out of the second-floor window.

"Who is it?" he shouted down to the front entrance.

Cash came into view and looked up at Dice.

"Hold up," Dice said, pulling back from the window. Cash stood there patiently until Dice returned.

"Yo," Dice said to get Cash's attention. Cash looked up and Dice tossed down the keys to the door.

A few seconds later Cash was letting himself into the apartment. He closed the door behind him and took a seat on the sofa. Dice sat on the other end of the sofa, rolling a blunt.

"What's up?" Dice asked, not looking up from what he was doing.

"'Sup," a very uneasy Cash said.

"So, where you been, man?"

"What happened to ya leg?" Cash asked, noticing that Dice's jeans were ripped at the bottom and he had bandages wrapped around his calf. Dice looked down at his leg.

"Oh, this? I got hit at the job we did tonight. Why you ain't show up?"

"Man, I had some other shit I needed to take care of. Where Click?"

"He went with them other cats to drop off the load of shit we lifted from Big Roy's spot." Dice ran his tongue along the edge of the blunt and pressed it firmly. "A-yo, that shit tonight was crazy! Nettie had us doing some *Mission Impossible* shit! Yo, I was like, what the fuck?" Dice rambled on about what went down. Cash sat listening, but not really listening.

He was thinking about some things he had on his mind that had been bothering him for a long time.

". . . the shit was crazy, man," Dice said, holding out the blunt to Cash. "You wanna hit this?"

Cash took the weed and inhaled deeply.

"So, what's up, man? What you want, coming over here this late?" Dice asked as he put up his leg on the arm of the sofa.

"Man, I want to tell you some shit that's going on, but I ain't tryna hear no bullshit, straight up. This is some serious shit."

Dice looked at Cash, ready to clown him, but then he

saw that the young boy was serious. He could tell that Cash was heavily burdened with something.

Cash began to tell Dice what he had been holding back. The two smoked and talked for about two hours.

"A'ight, Nett said her brother should be waiting right over here somewhere," Nate said, looking around. "Maybe he left because we're late."

Wild pulled the U-Haul over to the corner and put it in park. He kept the engine running and the two began to look around for James.

"FREEZE! Put your hands where I can see them!" several cops shouted with their guns drawn.

When Wild and Nate realized what was going on, they were already surrounded by police. Several seconds later, police cars began to pull up and box them in. They both put their hands in the air with bewildered looks on their faces. The doors opened and they both were yanked out of the U-Haul truck and thrown to the ground.

"Hold up, man! What the fuck?" Nate shouted as a knee from one of the officers was jammed in the back of his neck.

Brutal force was used on the two men as the officers searched them and handcuffed them. They were then dragged across the ground and over to the curb, where they were forced to sit. Police radios buzzed and hissed all around them. Wild and Nate looked at each other.

The U-Haul was being searched by several officers. Luckily, Click was nowhere in sight.

Detective Daniels walked over to the two men. He stood

in front of them, peering down with a smirk on his face. Nate looked at the detective with a screw face, but Wild smirked right back at the detective with confidence.

"What's poppin', fellas?" Detective Daniels asked, smiling down at them with his hands in his pockets. "What's your name?" he asked Wild.

"Lester Bonds," Wild lied nonchalantly.

"You got some ID stating that, Mr. Bonds?"

"I sure do." He continued to stare at Detective Daniels with a sinister grin.

Wild had all kinds of fake IDs and driver's licenses.

"What about you? What's your name?" he asked Nate.

"Lawyer," was all Nate said, looking at him stone-faced.

"Lawyer, huh?" The detective laughed. "If I find out that you got that truck filled with drugs, ain't no lawyer gonna be able to help you where you're going."

"Drugs?" Wild began to laughed. "Man, what you on? Ain't no drugs in that truck." He continued to laugh.

"Oh, so you trying to tell me that the both of you are moving at this time of night?" The detective looked at his watch.

Just then one of the officers came over to Detective Daniels.

"What you got?" Detective Daniels asked.

"Nothing," the officer said.

"Nothing! What do you mean, 'nothing'?" Detective Daniels asked.

"Nothing, sir. The truck is clean, inside and out."

"Did you check the door panels and underneath the truck?"

"Yes, sir," the officer answered.

"What about under the hood of the truck?" Detective Daniels was clearly pissed.

"We checked every inch of the truck, sir. There is nothing there." The officer walked away from the detective.

Detective Daniels looked back at Wild and Nate. Wild continued to smirk and Nate just sat there, mean-mugging the detective. He walked over to the truck to investigate it for himself. He got down onto the ground and looked under the truck. Daniels was irritated when he didn't find anything. Blist walked up to the truck.

"What's up?" Blist asked.

"Nothing! Not a goddamn thing!" Detective Daniels said as he got up off the ground. He rubbed his hand over his head and placed his hands in the pockets on his trench coat.

"What happened?" Blist asked.

"I got played is what happened. My informant told me there was going to be a truck load of drugs here." He walked away from Blist.

Blist followed behind him. "Looks like somebody else is paying your informant more."

"What?" Detective Daniels shouted, turning around to face Blist. "What are you talking about?"

Blist pulled Detective Daniels over to the side, out of earshot from the others.

"Rick, something doesn't smell right to me. You've been running in circles trying to solve these murders and now this. I think your informant set you up."

"No." Detective Daniels shook his head. "I've been working with him for years and I know one thing. He may not be loyal to anyone else, but he is loyal to me."

Blist shook his head and looked at him with disbelieving eyes.

"I'm surprised at you, Rick. You've been on these streets for years and you mean to tell me that you put your trust in a junkie? You're busy chasing everyone and catching no one. A junkie is only loyal to one thing—drugs! Your obsession with the job has caused you to lose focus." Blist walked away.

Detective Daniels stood there, staring off into the night. The veins on his neck began to expand. He hated to be made a fool of and his blood was boiling. An officer came over to him and interrupted his thoughts.

"Sir, what do you want to do with these two?" He pointed toward Nate and Wild.

The detective looked over at the men sitting on the curb.

"Oh, yeah, the captain wants you to call him," the officer added.

Detective Daniels exhaled heavily. That was all he needed. The captain would chew him out over this bogus sting. He'd wasted precious man hours, as well as overtime costs that some of the officers were putting in for the bust.

He had brought the information to the captain's attention when he first got the call from his informant. The captain wasn't interested because of where Detective Daniels had received his information. The captain felt it wasn't solid enough. But after forty-five minutes of reasoning with the captain, Detective Daniels finally convinced him to approve the bust. Now Daniels was going to be walking around with the seat of his pants missing, because the captain was definitely taking a chunk out of his ass when he talked to him.

"Sir?" the officer repeated.

"Check them for ID. If they don't have any, lock their asses up! Charge the driver with every vehicle violation in the book," Detective Daniels shouted as he walked away from the officer.

He walked past Wild and Nate, not looking their way one time. He went over to his truck, preparing to make the phone call to the captain. He looked at his watch, saw the time and knew the ass chewing was going to be even worse because of the late hour.

CHAPTER 36

Wild and Nate took the U-Haul to the rental station. They dropped the keys in the drop box and walked over to Nate's car, where Click sat waiting for them. The officer wasn't able to charge them with anything because they both had valid IDs. The truck was rented legally as well, so the police had to let them go.

"Yo, what happened?" Click asked.

After dropping off the shipment, Click told Wild and Nate that he was going to put gas in the car and that he would meet them at the U-Haul place. He knew they were going to meet up with Nettie's brother to tell him that there was a change in plans on him watching the stash.

"Man, the shit was crazy," Nate said, getting into the passenger's seat.

Nate had called Click after they were let go. Click had been blowing up his cell phone, calling to see where they were and why they were taking so long to meet him. But Nate couldn't answer the vibrating phone, at the time, because he was cuffed and sitting on the curb.

Wild sat in the backseat, quiet as a mouse. He was in deep thought. From experience, he hadn't felt comfortable leaving such a large amount of drugs in the hands of a fiend. He was actually quite surprised that Nettie would make a stupid move like that. The move discredited her ability to run such an organized team. He was already contemplating revenge on Nettie's brother. If no one else knew about Nettie meeting him there except Nettie and her brother, then her brother was a snitch.

Wild was a loner and made moves by himself. Hooking up with the team made him uncomfortable. There were too many people and stupid mistakes could cause someone to lose their life or to be jailed. Wild wasn't with either one.

"So tell me what happened, man." Click was amped.

"We got set up. That's what happened." Nate looked back at Wild.

"How you figure?" Click asked.

"Trust me, it was a setup, man." Nate didn't want to reveal too much information to Click until Wild talked to Nettie.

"A'ight, so who do you think did it?" Click asked.

"Don't know," Wild interjected.

"Do you think it was somebody from our team?" Click asked.

"Could be, could not be. Ya boy Cash ain't around, so who knows? But trust, I will find out," Wild said, almost demonically.

Click looked over at Nate who just shrugged his shoulders.

-◁-◁-◁-

"So tell me, Maria, what's the deal with you and Nettie?" Meat asked her.

They were sitting in the living room. They had been talking about the events of the night since everyone left.

"What do you mean, Meat?"

"I mean, I know, Nettie. Are you and Nettie . . . you know?" he asked, already knowing the answer.

"What do you think, Meat?"

"Well, at first I did think that you two were lovers. But then when you and I became close and you made love to me I figured maybe you were just roommates."

"Honestly? Yes, Meat, we were sexually active with each other. I love Netta, but lately my *sensaciones*, they're different."

"Huh?" Meat looked at her strangely not understanding the Spanish word she used.

"Oh, sorry Meat. I was talking about my *feelings*. Ever since meeting you, my feelings for Netta have changed. I think I'm falling in love with you, Meat."

Meat gazed into her eyes, pulled her close and they kissed passionately.

By the time Wild got to the hotel it was already after seven a.m. Nettie was lying in the bed, sound asleep. He knocked on the room door and waited. Finally Nettie opened the door and stood there in her red lace bra and thong. She walked back over to the bed.

"How'd it go?" she asked him, climbing back into bed.

Wild sat down on the bed and looked at her.

"What?" She rubbed her eyes.

"We had a problem."

"I was wondering what took you so long. What happened?" She sat up and crossed her legs.

"It was a setup, Nettie. The cops knew we were going to be there. They were waiting for us."

"What?" she shouted. "So how did you get outta there? Don't tell me you killed a cop?"

"Naw—"

"So what happened?" She cut him off before he could finish his sentence.

"Calm down and let me talk. We was waiting for your brother and they rolled up on us, ten deep. They searched the truck and came up with nothing."

"Nothing? How is that possible?"

"Because I dropped off the load with my man I told you about." He looked at her for a reaction.

"You what? What are you talking about? I told you I had a spot already, Wild." She got slick with him.

"Hold up. If I hadn't done what I did, me and Nate would be locked up and ya shit would be police evidence to put us away for life."

Nettie sat there, glaring at him. Then it all registered. She softened her eyes and put her hands over her face.

"My bad," she said as an attempt to apologize.

"That's your way of saying you're sorry?" He couldn't believe her.

"I'm sorry, Wild, I just—"

"Go off without thinking." He finished her sentence for her.

"Yeah, I guess you can say that."

"Nettie, listen, I think ya brother dropped a dime."

"What?" her attitude reappeared.

"Yeah. How else would the cops have known we would be at that exact location?"

"I don't know, but I know it ain't my brother. My brother is a lot of things, but he aint no snitch!" She rolled her eyes at him.

"Ya brother is a fiend, Nettie. Come on, you can't be serious." He tried to reason with her.

"You don't know shit about my brother!"

"I know enough to know you don't let an addict watch drugs. What do you think he would've done, Nettie?" Wild turned around to face her.

"He wouldn't have touched a damn thing, especially if I told him not to."

"You have a lot of confidence in ya brother. You obviously don't know much about a fiend. They don't care about family when they want that next blast, Nettie," he said.

"Wild, I don't need you to school me on shit. I've been on them streets for a long time."

"A'ight, babe, I understand. Just calm down. So who do you think snitched, because somebody did."

"I don't know." She pouted as she thought.

"Do you think Cash said something?"

"No, Wild, Cash ain't like that, either. Just let it go. We still got the shit and nobody got hurt or locked up." She looked up at him.

"This time. What about next time?" he asked.

"There won't be a next time. We will have a meeting,

because obviously somebody ran their mouth." And Nettie was satisfied with that.

Wild lay back on the bed. She just didn't get it. Nate was right: Nettie was stubborn. But what Nettie didn't know was that Wild was just as stubborn. He wanted what he wanted when he wanted it. The monster in him that he managed to keep at bay was now beginning to surface.

CHAPTER 37

Turmoil and destruction washed over the city. Leroy Jenkins let the dogs out after his second stash house had been robbed. Leroy didn't take any shorts. He sent his men out to terrorize the city, beating down anybody in the business, trying to find out information on who could have robbed him a second time. He even gave Nate and his crew a promotion to lead a team of men out on the hunt.

They broke down doors and shot up luxury cars owned by others in the business. Leroy was elated with their actions because he wanted to make a statement. Truth be told he saw his operation falling apart at the seams. And to add insult to injury, it was hurting his street status. At this point, he was going to use any and everyone he could to set an example not to fuck with Leroy Jenkins.

Two weeks later

TJ and Tyler were back on the block and the product was flowing lovely throughout the hood. Dice was back on his feet. He and Click had recruited a few more young teens and set them up on another block. Most of the small-time hustlers knew who they were and their history, so taking over the major areas was an easy task for them. The dealers simply bowed out gracefully, giving up the territories without putting up a fight, because they thought it was for Leroy.

Everyone in Nettie's crew was getting along well. All eleven of them would, at times, meet over Nettie's or Nate's houses to kick it. They drank, smoked and laughed as a family—all except Wild. He always played the back.

Wild had let Nettie believe the incident with the cops was squashed when, in reality, he was waiting for the right time to take care of the snitching problem. Wild was like a hawk, circling his prey quietly. He was always mindful and kept a watchful eye on anyone he came in contact with. But Nettie was in his heart and they had the same vision in sight. He wanted Leroy, and so did she. Nettie had something he didn't have and that was a crew to help her pull it off. Wild pretty much stayed to himself except when he and Nettie were alone. They counted money together and continued to spend time with each other, mostly discussing their plans to shut down Leroy permanently.

Nate made sure he continued to play Leroy close so they could easily tear him down when the time came.

"What's good, Big Roy?" Nate asked Leroy.

Leroy had called Nate to his office for a meeting. Nate shook Leroy's hand and took a seat in the chair.

"Whatchu know, young blood?"

"Chillin', man," Nate responded.

"I know I haven't been myself, but when a nigga fucks with me or mine, it takes me to a different place. You see, son, I've been walking this planet for a long time. I put in my time and I've established a lot of businesses to give these motherfuckers jobs. Somebody gonna pay for this shit and, until I find out who did this, everybody's gonna suffer until somebody drops a dime. You feel me?"

Nate nodded his head.

"I was scheduled to go on a trip south when this shit went down. I still need to take my trip, but I ain't leaving until I feel comfortable that I got somebody in place that can handle things while I'm gone."

"I hear you, Big Roy,"

"So I've decided to leave you and Dak to run things. I got a few good men that can back the two of you. Dak's been with me for a long time, so he knows the ins and outs, but you are young and you got brains. You're up with the times and know how to mix it up with the new breed out here."

Nate sat there with a serious look on his face, as if he was contemplating things. But, in reality, he was thinking that with Leroy out of town, this would be the perfect opportunity to eliminate his whole operation.

"That's what's up, Big Roy. I got ya back."

"I know you do, son. I see why Ishmael took care of you and the rest. He used to tell me all the time he had a good crew. I used to laugh in his face, but now I see." Leroy shook his head.

"Yeah, Ish was good peoples," Nate said, remembering him.

Dak walked into the room. He gave Nate dap and took

a seat next to him.

"All right, now that Dak is here, let me put you two up on what I need done 'round here while I'm gone. Then I'm gonna have a meeting with the others and let them know they take their orders from you two." He pointed at both of them.

Both Nate and Dak looked at each other then back to Leroy.

"Nate, let me ask you something," Leroy said.

"What's up?"

"I heard there's a female that's doing a little something in the streets. I don't know her name, but I know she's not buying weight from me. I heard the product she pushing comes close to mine. You know anything about this?"

"Naw, Roy, but let me put some people on it and see what I can dig up for ya," Nate said, showing no emotion.

"That's my man." Leroy held his hand out for a shake.

Yuming, Shawnee, Jasmine, and Marisa were sitting in Yuming's apartment. Shawnee had called this meeting with the ladies behind Nettie's back.

"Damn, Yuming, it looks like a Chinese garden in here." Jasmine commented on Yuming's apartment.

She had colorful throw pillows on the floor, on one sofa and had all kinds of Chinese plants decorating the room. There was a huge, fifty-gallon, saltwater fish tank with colorful tropical fish and ancient Chinese lamps. It really looked like a tropical garden.

"Shawnee, how you gonna call a meeting and not have it at your place?" Jasmine asked.

"Because my man is home and it ain't none of his business what I'm doing with y'all. He's already starting to get on my damn nerves now." She rolled her eyes.

"What's going on?" Marisa wanted to know.

"Girl, this whack ass nigga thinks I'm out here fucking somebody else because he noticed I been buying a lot of new shit."

"So?" Yuming asked.

"So? Bitch, that nigga know ain't that much stripping in the world that's gonna get me a Lexus," Shawnee said with much attitude.

"Well, chica, you the loco one to buy a Lexus in the first place. Shit, I didn't even go out and buy something like that," Jasmine told her.

"Fuck that! I put in work for that money, so why can't I buy what the fuck I want?"

"Because Nettie said not to ball out spending money, calling attention to yourself, Shawnee," Yuming reminded her.

"Fuck, Nettie! She bought her a new whip, furs, and shit. Why can't we spend our money the way we want?"

The ladies shook their heads but didn't say a word.

"Speaking of money, that's why I wanted us to meet. I want to talk about that," Shawnee said.

"About what?" Marisa asked.

"About whether we're getting our fair share of the loot. I mean, it's eleven of us and how we know we getting broke off proper? This Wild dude walks up in the picture and all of a sudden, he running shit. What the fuck is that?" Shawnee asked.

"Yeah, I was peeping that myself," Jasmine said, shaking her head.

"And what's fuckin' with me is that Nettie just letting this nigga take over. What was the oath? Money over dick." Shawnee looked into each of their faces, making sure she had their attention. "That bitch straight up said she would kill us if we broke an oath. That bitch was ready to cut our throats with that razor she keeps in her mouth."

"Maria said she don't carry the blade anymore. She says she keeps a gun now," Marisa said.

"I don't give a fuck! I got a gun, too," Shawnee shouted. She lifted her skirt, revealing a .22 strapped to her leg. "So what you saying?"

"Easy, Shawnee! Tranquillo, calm down." Jasmine tried to calm her. "You so sensitive."

"You damn right I am! You can't tell me y'all not feeling me? Money over niggas, was what she said. Ain't no dick worth losing paper over, right?" She looked at each of them.

They all looked at each other in agreement, except Yuming.

"Okay. So what if Wild's dickin' her down good?" Yuming responded. "Sometimes a bitch needs that, but Nettie still hasn't lost her focus on what she's doing. She still makes shit happen. She still pays us, regardless of how much you think she's getting. She's still hitting us off proper like, making our pockets deep." Yuming voiced her opinion in Nettie's defense.

"But our pockets don't run as deep as hers," Shawnee said.

"Shawnee you're being selfish and greedy," Yuming told her.

"Yuming, please, Okay? You just be glad that we let your Chinese ass be down, that's all. So don't come at me with the bullshit." Shawnee blew her off.

"You don't want this, Shawnee," Yuming warned her with a serious look, making her eyes look like slits on her face.

"Bring it, Yuming." Shawnee lifted her skirt to show the gun. "That karate shit ain't gonna stop no bullet."

"You sure about that, Shawnee?" Yuming continued to glare at her, scowling.

"All right, stop it! Oh ¡Dios mio! We supposed to be together, not fighting each other," Jasmine jumped in.

Shawnee lowered her skirt and sat back on the sofa. Yuming continued to glare at her.

"OK, so what are we going to do?" Jasmine asked.

"I think we should call a meeting with Nettie and just tell her how we feel," Shawnee said.

"Oh, Dios mio, estás loco? Nettie would kill us all dead if we came to her like that," Jasmine said.

"She's right, Shawnee," Marisa agreed.

Yuming didn't say a word, but Shawnee spoke up.

"OK, so what do y'all say we do? Because something's got to be said to her about how we feel."

"You say something, Shawnee. You're the one who brought this to our attention," Yuming suggested.

"I don't give a fuck! I'll tell her. It ain't no thing for me."

"So you gonna speak for yourself, right?" Marisa asked, really not wanting to approach Nettie.

"I ain't scared of Nettie, Marisa. She bleeds just like I do," Shawnee said.

"I hope you're ready to feel Nettie's wrath. Speak for yourself and don't put my name in it," Yuming said.

"Whatever. Nettie don't move no mountains over here," Shawnee proclaimed.

❖ ❖ ❖

Jasmine and Marisa were sitting in the car in front of the apartment they shared.

"So, Marisa, what do you think about Shawnee?" Jasmine asked.

"Mi hermana, I don't know 'bout that girl. She is shady, you know?" Marisa responded.

"Sí, I feel you. She didn't even invite Maria to the meeting, you know?"

"Sí. I think we need to tell our cousin what's going on. You never know, that girl might be trying to set up Maria too."

Jasmine nodded her head in agreement and started the car, heading for their cousin's house.

CHAPTER 38

Little Cash sat in his bedroom, staring at a picture of his mother when she was younger. She was a beauty queen at a young age. A knock came at his door and he got up to answer it. He opened it and his mother stood there, looking thirty years older than the picture. She was stricken with cancer and her body was being eaten away by the deadly disease. His mother walked with a cane. He stepped to the side to let her into the room. Little Cash watched her as she grimaced in pain with each step. She walked over to his bed and sat down, blowing air from her mouth with relief after standing so long on her sore limbs.

Little Cash sat next to his mother on the bed.

"You all right, Ma?"

"Yes, son, I'm as good as to be expected."

"What's on ya mind, Ma?" he asked, knowing that his mother hardly ever came into his room. He knew she was there for a reason.

"I wanted to talk to you, son, about what you will do when I'm gone."

"Ma, stop talking like that!" Little Cash said, putting his

face into his hands. She reached over and rubbed his back.

"Son, the reality is that I am not going to be here much longer. Pretty soon I am going to have to go into the hospital. I can almost feel the cancer spreading. You already know that there is nothing they can do for me and I don't want hospice here. I don't want my kids to have to look at me every day in this house, suffering until I die."

Little Cash got up from the bed and walked over to the window.

"Darrell." She called him by his birth name. "I know you don't want to hear this, but this is life, son. That's why I tried to talk to you as you were growing up. But I realized I couldn't teach you to be a man, and I had to let you go out and learn the best way you could. I just prayed that the things I said to you would stick in your head and you would use it. But son, I need you to step up more than ever. Your brothers and sister are going to need you and running those streets is not the way. You are still young and it is not too late for you to do something with your life. You have a high school diploma and I'm proud of that but it is not enough in this day and age."

Little Cash turned to look at his mother and his eyes were wet with tears.

"Come here, Darrell." She patted the bed next to her.

He walked back over to the bed and sat next to her.

"I know this is a lot of pressure for you but selling drugs is not the life that you should be living. I pray for you every day, son."

Little Cash looked at his mother with wide eyes.

"You know I sell drugs?" he asked her in disbelief. His

mother laughed.

"Boy, I'm sick, not dumb. I've known for a long time but I knew I couldn't stop you because you would only sneak out and still do it. I know about your friend Ishmael, too. I know you don't want to end up like him, do you?"

He shook his head, no.

"Ma, I have been thinking about doing something different with my life, because things haven't been the same since he died. He was good to me, Ma. He talked to me about life and he told me I was too young to be out on the streets. He used to tell me I was smart. To be honest with you, Ma, I've kinda backed away from it because too many people are getting hurt. That's not me, Ma. I don't hurt people. Haven't you noticed I've been home more?"

"Yes, I have, but I also know something is not right with you either." She looked at him.

"I got a lot on my mind and I'm tryna find out which way I'm going next, without causing myself to get killed. I want to clean up my life, but we need the money to live. If something happens to you, then it's all on me to take care of them."

She rubbed his arm and smiled at him.

"I know you will make the right decision. I love you, son and I know you will do the right thing."

CHAPTER 39

Janet was on a rampage around the house. Tyler had been missing school and she finally found the notices. She had been doing so much overtime at work. When she came in at night it was early in the morning and he would be asleep. When she woke up in the morning he would already be gone, and she figured he was at school. She was off work today and had just come from Tyler's room after looking through his things. She found boxes of new sneakers way in the back of his closet and mounds of new clothes with the tags still on them. Some of the clothes cost one hundred dollars or more for a pair of jeans.

Janet was enraged, knowing the reason he was able to afford such expensive garments. She went through his drawers and saw photos of naked girls. She also found a nine-millimeter gun underneath his mattress. That was the straw that broke the camel's back.

Janet ran out the house and got into her hooptie, an old Dodge Intrepid. She raced through the streets, stopping at each corner that the young hustlers stood on.

Meanwhile, Tyler was hugging the block with a couple

of new recruits. Click had put him in charge of the boys. TJ was in school and would join him later. His Uncle James walked up on the corner and approached him. He had found out that Tyler was putting in work and often came by to cop from his nephew or ask him for free drugs. James he had no clue that his nephew was working for his sister. Tyler would oblige his uncle every time he asked for money or product because he loved his uncle, despite his condition.

"Hey, unc."

"What's going on, nephew? You got something for your old unc?" James smiled with a yellow-toothed grin.

"Yeah, unc, hold up a minute." Tyler walked off.

Janet pulled up to the corner and rolled down her window.

"James," she yelled out.

James looked over at her and turned his back to her.

"James! Come on, this is important!"

Tyler was coming from around a house where they had their stash when he saw his mother at the corner. He stepped back out of her view.

"What, Janet?" James asked nonchalantly.

"Have you seen Tyler?"

"Why?"

Janet got out of the car and walked over to him.

"James, have you seen my son out here?"

"You asked me that already," he said.

"You never answered my question, James. He has been missing school and I found a gun in his drawer. I know he's out in these streets selling drugs. If you cared about your nephew, you wouldn't want him to fall victim to these streets," she said with hurt in her voice.

James looked at his sister and he could see the hurt in her eyes.

"I understand, Janet, but I ain't seen him. If I do see him, I'll make sure I talk to him and then send him home."

"Thank you, James. I don't want to lose my baby to that lifestyle. He aint built for this."

"I know, sis. I hear you." He looked down at the ground.

She began to walk back over to her car and then she turned around.

"James, I'm sorry about what happened last month at the house." She got in her car and drove off.

Tyler walked back to the corner with the heroin package for his uncle.

"Here, unc. What did my mother want?" Tyler asked, already knowing the answer.

James wanted to tell his nephew about the street life. He knew the road he was traveling was the wrong road. He wanted to advise Tyler to turn and go home and be a teenager. But who was he to tell Tyler about living the wrong life? He was the drug addict that couldn't get his own life together. So, instead of giving his nephew good advice, he looked at the three pills of heroin he held in his hand. He thanked Tyler, gave him dap and moved on, never answering his question.

Nettie pulled up to the club in her brand-new convertible BMW. She got out of the car wearing her full-length chinchilla coat with the hat to match. She walked into the club and went to the owner and asked him to let her and Maria have a minute alone to talk. He agreed and notified the dancers to stay out of the dressing room for a few moments. Nettie walked into the dressing room where Maria was alone and getting dressed for her shift

"What's up, Maria?" she asked her.

Maria looked Nettie up and down.

"¿Que pasa, Netta?" she asked dryly.

"You tell me." Nettie eyed her.

"What you wanna know?" Maria continued to put her make-up on, never looking up at her.

Nettie leaned up against the vanity table and put her hands on her hips.

"So, what's up with you and Meat?"

Maria looked up at Nettie.

"¿Que?"

"What nothing, Maria. You heard me. You fuckin' Meat?" Maria stood to her feet and brushed past Nettie.

"Netta, please, okay? You don't even come home anymore, so how do you know what I'm doing?"

"I peeped ya game. Let me explain something to you: Meat is off limits. You don't fuck with him. You feel me?"

Maria stared at Nettie like she was crazy.

"You got a lot of nerve," Maria said, bobbing her head back and forth. "You around here screwing everything that moves, man or woman, and you got the nerve to tell me who I can screw?" Maria waved her hand at Nettie and rolled her eyes. "You think I don't know, Netta? I know everything that you're doing." She turned her back on Nettie to continue to get dressed.

Before Maria knew what happened, Nettie had grabbed around her throat and a nine pressed to her temple.

"You obviously forgot who the fuck I am. I'm dat bitch," she said as spittle flew from her mouth, hitting Maria on the face. "You listen to me, bitch. I own you, Maria, and don't you ever forget that. You do what I say, when I say." Nettie was in a jealous rage and breathing hard.

It was true that Nettie had become out of control since the money started rolling in. She was tricking her money off like no tomorrow. She began to let her steadily-rising status go to her head. She would have sex sessions with Wild and sometimes up to five women at a time. She treated Maria like crap and until recently, Nettie had no clue that Maria had moved in with Meat. When Nettie got word that Meat was breaking Maria off, she became jealous. Nettie didn't want Meat for herself, but he had always been loyal to her. Now that he was with Maria, she felt that she was not in control.

"¡No puedo creerle, Netta! I can't believe you!"

"You remember who I am now, don't you?" Nettie whispered.

Maria could barely breathe. She was sweating and tears fell from her eyes, but no sound came out of her mouth. The sinister look in Nettie's eyes made her fear for her life.

"Stay away from Meat. He ain't for you." She released Maria's neck and put the gun away. Nettie kissed Maria hard on the mouth. She backed up and looked at herself in the mirror, brushing her hand over her already neat hair and sashayed out of the dressing room.

Maria stood there with her chest heaving, trying to calm

herself. She wondered why none of the other girls came into the dressing room. Hatred for Nettie seemed to build with each breath she took. She was going to make Nettie pay for what she did, if it was the last thing she did.

CHAPTER 40

Since Little Cash had spoken with his mother, he felt the need to clean up his life. He knew his mother wasn't going to live forever and with her disease progressing, he knew it could be only a matter of a couple months before she died. His siblings were going to need him and he knew living the life he did was not guaranteed.

Little Cash confided in Dice and told him something that had been on his mind since going over to Nettie's house that day but Dice didn't believe him. He'd asked Dice not to say anything to the others, but little did he know that Dice was spilling his guts at that very moment.

"Go 'head with the bullshit, Dice," Nate said as he ate a cheese steak sandwich.

"Naw, man, I'm dead ass serious. Kid came to the crib and was about to cry, telling me what he saw," Dice said, trying to convince Nate.

"So what, you believe him?" Nate looked up at Dice.

"All I'm saying is, let's go check it out."

"For what, Dice? Y'all niggas be trippin' off that weed. Ish is dead, man. Why y'all can't let his soul rest?" he asked with a mouth full of sandwich.

Dice sat there in the chair and watched Nate wolf down his sandwich.

"Oh yeah, y'all niggas need to meet Nettie at her spot tomorrow night. It's about to be on! We gonna put an end to Big Roy's operation while he out of town," Nate said while putting the scraps in the trash can. He still held a small piece of the sandwich in his hand.

"Word?" Dice asked.

"Word, it's going down."

"That's what's up. So who gonna lullaby Big Roy?"

"Man, that don't even matter. That nigga ain't shit without his boys." Nate shoved the last of his sandwich into his mouth. "I gotta get ready to go hook up with Dak while Leroy is gone."

"Word," was all that Dice said, but he had been thinking about what Little Cash told him that night he came to his crib.

Detective Daniels's cell phone began to ring. He was cruising the streets, looking for his informant. He had not been able to catch up with him since they ran up on Nate and Wild that night. He had been struggling with the idea of his informant of several years was feeding him bogus information. He still couldn't believe that his informant would do that. He had been on point every time Detective Daniels needed him and had never slipped him false information.

He looked at the call indicator on his phone and flipped open the lid.

"Daniels," he said into the phone. "What you got, Sam?"

He sat there with a blank look on his face as Sam relayed the information about the partial finger print linking to Beverly's murder.

Sam was telling him what his heart didn't want to hear.

"Thanks, Sam. I owe you big time," he said. "Yeah, I'm gonna be okay. I gotta do what I gotta do and I can't worry about my personal feelings right now. This person committed a murder and they need to be punished for it."

Detective Daniels disconnected the call. He laid his head back on the headrest and closed his eyes.

Wild sat in his rental car. Although he was now getting money, he still chose to rent various cars to get around. Nettie told him she couldn't understand why he continued to rent cars when he was making enough money that he could just buy one and pay cash. But Wild wasn't into tricking his money.

He had been out cruising all day, watching their blocks. Now he was watching the blocks where TJ and Tyler were working. As scheduled, TJ had arrived after doing his homework. Wild and Nettie were supposed to link up and engage in some much needed stress relieving sex. He told her that he had something to do and would call when he was on his way.

Nettie had become more submissive to Wild, per his request. She allowed him to completely make the decisions for the crew. Wild was confident and knew that he had Nettie where he wanted her. Wild had Nettie turned out, this was no easy task. But Wild knew how to eat pussy, locking down on her clit, and that always sent her into a frenzy. With Nettie under control, he vowed to be the next King of Essex County.

The boys continued to oversee the block as their newly assigned runners did the work. James walked back onto the corner and approached Tyler. They talked for a minute before Tyler handed him the drugs. Wild kept a watchful eye, and saw that no money exchanged hands for the drugs. James walked off at a quick pace and disappeared up the street.

Nettie walked into her mother's house and stopped in the living room. Janet was sitting on the couch, rocking back and forth. She looked up with red and puffy eyes and saw Nettie standing there.

"What's wrong with you?" Nettie asked with attitude.

"Now is not the time, Nettie." Janet sniffed and wiped her eyes with the back of her hand.

"No, for real. What's wrong?" Nettie softened her voice, seeing that her sister was seriously hurting. She thought maybe something had happened to her mother, or one of the kids.

"Where's Ma?" Nettie asked.

"She's in the bed."

"Where's the kids?"

"Naeesha and the baby is 'sleep, and I don't know where Tyler is," Janet responded and began to cry again.

Nettie walked over to her sister and sat next to her.

"What do you mean, you don't know where he is?"

"Like I said, I don't know where he is, but I found this under the mattress in his room." She pulled the gun from her purse and showed Nettie.

Nettie looked at the gun, wide-eyed. It was the gun that she had took from Maria and used to shoot Stacks on the first robbery. It was the same gun that had at least three bodies on it. It was also one of the gun that she gave Dice when he said he needed guns for the new recruits. Nettie had given Dice the gun because she went out and bought new ones for herself. She had different guns to go to the shooting range and others she carried from day to day. But this gun, she knew too well.

"Where'd he get it from?"

"Nettie, I don't know, I don't even know where he is."

Nettie sat there, heavy in thought, not saying a word. Now how would Tyler get his hands on a gun like that? Did Dice give the gun to him or did he buy the gun from whom ever Dice did give it too? Who would sell a kid a gun? Where would he get the money from to pay for it and why would he need it? Most importantly, how could he get that particular gun? She knew Dice wouldn't be stupid enough to give her nephew the gun, he didn't even know Tyler. All of these thoughts went through Nettie's mind.

She never once thought about how easy it was to get a gun. Nor did she ever think that her own nephew could fall victim to the streets, just like every other teen out there. This hit close to home and she was now looking at the situation differently.

The two women sat there side by side while Janet cried. Nettie thought of her next move.

"I saw James today and I asked him to look out for him. He told me he would send him home if he saw him. But he hasn't come home yet and I've been out looking for him all day. I got a letter from the school that he has missed almost two weeks of school. Something happened to him. I just know it!" Janet began to cry all over again.

"Ain't nothing happened to him, Janet. Stop talking like that." Nettie rubbed her back.

This was the first time in, a while, that the sisters actually had any physical contact or spoke to each other without arguing.

"I'm gonna go look for him. I know people, so we will find him. Don't worry about it, okay?" Nettie assured Janet and stood up.

"It ain't that easy, Nettie. That's my son, you don't understand how I feel," Janet said through her stuffed nose.

"Yeah, I do understand. That's my nephew and I love him, too." Nettie turned and stormed out of the house without saying another word.

CHAPTER 41

The building was abandoned but the fiends still lived there. It was night time and they still dwelled in the darkness, using candles as their light. James moved aside the board that covered the door to the abandoned house. He squeezed his narrow frame through it and went inside and followed the glow from the candles. When he reached the candlelit room, there were three other fiends there. They were sitting on an old mattress, smoking crack. Neither of the two men and woman looked up to acknowledge him.

James found his usual spot in the corner and retrieved the works from his jeans pocket. He prepared to cook the dope when a shadow appeared in front of him.

"I'm not sharing, so step off," he said, not looking up at the body that stood before him. He thought it was one of the fiends that would sometimes beg him for a hit whenever he got his heroin.

But when the fiend didn't move like he usually did, James looked up. The man standing before him was holding a gun and it was pointed right at him.

"Yo, man, what you doing?" James asked, almost dropping

his dope to the floor.

"You's a snitch bitch," the raspy voice said.

"What? What are you talking about? I ain't no snitch," James said as the warm liquid of urine began to wet his pants.

The man cocked the gun and aimed it at James's head.

"Wait a minute!" James held out his hand to protest.

This time the two males and female fiends that were smoking the crack cocaine looked up to see what was going on. They all jumped to their feet, startled as they realized the man had a gun.

Nettie drove through the streets, stopping at every block that anybody stood on, asking of her nephew's whereabouts. No one could say that they had seen him. Her mind was racing as she began to think the inevitable might be true. She didn't want to believe that her own nephew had been recruited to work for her. Her twisted mind was almost wishing that something else had happened to him; anything except Tyler selling drugs for her. She continued to drive and search for Tyler.

Janet put on her coat and left the house. She could no longer sit there and wait for her son to come home. Janet really believed that he would never come back and she had to keep looking for him. She jumped into her car and raced up the street to trace the route she had driven earlier that evening. She was hoping and praying nothing had happened to her son, but her heart was telling her different.

Detective Daniels pulled his truck in front of the house of the convict that he was preparing to arrest. He desperately wished that it was someone different. He looked up at the house and saw that there were no lights on. He knew that someone was in the house because someone was always home. But the car of the murderer was not there. He figured maybe they had to work late, but he was prepared to wait it out. He made a phone call to Blist to tell him of his findings. Blist insisted that he not be the one to make the arrest. He tried to convince Detective Daniels to let him make the arrest instead. But Detective Daniels was adamant about his decision to handle it on his own and with no backup. He sat there in front of the house and waited.

TJ and Tyler were posted up against the building when Nettie turned onto the block. Tyler didn't know that it was Nettie because he hadn't seen her since she purchased the new whip.

"Damn, look at that joint right there," Tyler said, admiring the car.

"Yeah, that shit is fly," TJ agreed.

She pulled her car to the curb and got out. When Tyler realized who she was, it was too late.

"Hey, auntie," he said, all of sudden going back to his old self.

Even TJ had to looked at him cross-eyed to make sure he heard right.

"Please tell me," Nettie said, stepping up onto the sidewalk and approaching him, "please tell me you ain't out here puttin' in work, Tyler?"

"What are you talking about, Aunt Nettie?" He was shaking in his sneakers.

She looked over and noticed TJ. Her eyes became wide.

"You too?" she asked him, shocked.

TJ just lowered his head, avoiding eye contact.

"Hell no, both of y'all get ya asses home now. Ain't no way in hell I'ma let the streets get y'all too."

"Aunt Nettie, ain't nothing wrong with making a little money. You used to say that all the time," Tyler tried to reason.

"Boy, are you nuts? I was talking about me. This life ain't for y'all."

Nettie now knew that they were working for her. She saw the dope that the younger runners were selling. They would sell the drugs and then bring TJ and Tyler the money. Nettie knew what her packages looked like and she felt like she had failed her nephew. She always knew he would be something great in life, because he was a straight-A student. Now Nettie knew that she was the one who had put him onto the street life. It was almost too much. Tyler had always marveled at how Nettie had nice cars and fine clothes, but she never thought that the material things would cloud his brain.

"No, to hell with this! Shop is closed," she told him and TJ.

A female screaming made everyone look up the street in that direction. Two male fiends carried James's body. They were trying to run, but the dead weight was slowing them down. The female fiend was screaming at the top of her lungs.

"Call an ambulance! Somebody shot Black Santa!" she repeated over and over.

Nettie felt her heart speed up. The woman was screaming her brother's name. Was that her brother's body they were carrying? She took off running with Tyler and TJ on her heels.

Nettie could see a dark figure making his way up the street. She wasn't certain of what she saw because it was dark, but she thought she recognized the body shape. With her mind racing after hearing her brother's street name being yelled out, she could have been mistaken.

Once they reached the body, the fiends laid him down on the ground. Nettie's hands began to shake as she saw the blood leaking from two holes in her brother's chest and one in his forehead. Tyler dropped to his knees and began to cry like a baby. TJ stood there, stone-faced, as he remembered his mother. Tears streamed from Nettie's face. She looked up the street again and the person had vanished. The wheels began to turn in her head. It was total chaos on the streets that night. Everyone knew and liked Black Santa.

Nettie began to question the fiends, asking who had done this to her brother. She was frantic and losing self-control. She pulled out her gun and began to threaten them because they couldn't tell her who came into the smoke house and killed her brother. They could only give her a slight description, which wasn't much due to the minimal lighting in the house.

CHAPTER 42

The hissing from Detective Daniels's police radio came to life.

"Car two-two-seven."

"Car two-two-seven," he said.

"Car two-two-seven," the radio hissed. "Code 10-71 on the eight hundred block of Eighteenth Avenue. EMTs on the way. Code two. I repeat, code two!"

"Two-two-seven in route!" Detective Daniels threw on his siren and screeched out of the parking space.

Sirens could be heard in the distance. The dealers began to move off the streets.

"Tyler, you and TJ get outta here now! Go home!" Nettie commanded them, her eyes wet.

TJ had to practically drag Tyler from the ground. The two boys walked up the block, away from the corner. Nettie stood and brushed her coat. It was stained with her brother's blood, but she didn't care. She walked over to her car and got in. She pulled off down the street and drove right past

Detective Daniels. They both looked each other in the face as they passed one another. Detective Daniels almost sideswiped a car. He pulled the wheel hard to the left to avoid the parked car. He looked in his rearview mirror and saw the tail lights of the Beamer disappearing around the corner.

He was deep in thought as he pulled up to where two other police cars had gotten to the scene before him. He hopped out of his car and walked over to the body that lay on the ground. The female fiend was sitting on the ground not far from the body, crying. One of the officers went over to her to question her. Once Detective Daniels reached the body, he dropped his head. He turned his back and began to pace in a semi-circle.

Blist pulled up in his car just as the ambulance arrived. The workers jumped out of the truck and rushed over to the body with their medical equipment in their hands. Blist walked up to Detective Daniels and saw the look on his face.

"You all right?" he asked.

"Yeah." Detective Daniels sighed.

"Did you make the arrest?" Blist was more concerned about the arrest than the dead body lying on the ground.

"No." Detective Daniels walked back over to the body and the EMTs were now calling the morgue. They advised that they were bringing in a body, DOA.

Blist looked down at the body.

"Looks like another one bites the dust. He probably stole a stash or sold a burn bag."

"Shit!" Detective Daniels yelled out in defeat.

Everyone on the scene looked in his direction.

"Rick, what's up, man?" Blist asked.

"That was my informant." Detective Daniels pointed at James.

Blist looked at the body and then back at the detective.

"This was your CI?"

Detective Daniels nodded. He put his hands behind his head and interlocked his fingers.

"So who do you think did it?" Blist asked.

"Not sure, Dave, but this shit is getting out of control. I got bodies dropping out of the sky and no one to pin them on." He looked defeated.

"Why don't you go home and get a good night's rest? I'll finish up here," Blist offered.

"No, I wouldn't be able to sleep anyway. You can finish up here. I'm going back to wait for the suspect."

"Rick, you are going to blow a gasket. You're gonna have to slow down sooner or later. This thing will eventually blow up in your face. I've seen it a hundred times. Step back and take a look at the situation and then assess it." Blist tried to offer his partner some advice.

"I'm not gonna sit still while lives are being lost on my streets!" Daniels said and walked off toward his truck.

Blist stood there and watched him.

"That's a time bomb waiting to blow," he said to no one in particular.

CHAPTER 43

Nettie drove at excessive speeds through the city streets, enraged. She called Maria on her cell phone and she didn't answer. She called Nate, but he couldn't talk because he was with Dak. She knew she couldn't blow his cover, so she hung up. Next she called Wild.

"What's up, baby?" he asked when he answered.

"Where are you?" she asked, sounding out of breath.

"I'm at Bodilicious. What's the matter?" he asked, detecting her uneasiness.

Nettie tried to control herself. "They shot my brother," she blurted out as the tears began to pour from her eyes.

"Calm down, baby. Where are you?"

"I'm coming down by the club now. I need you right now. I am so mad I could kill all these muthafuckas out here!" She was losing control.

"No. Nettie, pull the car over now and stay right there. I'm coming for you." He disconnected the call.

She continued to drive because she was only a block away from the club. She saw Wild exit the club just as she pulled over at the corner. She blew the horn to get his attention. He turned, spotted her and jogged over to the car. He opened the driver's side door.

"Get out," he said.

She looked up at him with red eyes, reluctant to get out of the car.

"Nettie, get out of the car. What is wrong with you, driving around like this?" He was serious.

She got out of the car and he embraced her. She held on to him as the tears continued to flow. He walked her around the car and helped her into the passenger's seat. After he jumped behind the wheel, he reached over and pulled her close, giving her another hug and a kiss to the forehead.

As they drove Nettie told Wild about what had just took place moments earlier. She also told him how she was employing her nephew and his friend. She expressed to him that she never would have intentionally involved her nephew and his friend. Nettie talked about how she was enraged and thought there were shady individuals right under their noses within the crew. She mentioned that Maria had been acting funny lately and then what she found out about her and Meat.

Nettie was furious as well as hurt. She was a sensitive type of woman and if her feelings were hurt, she retaliated by inflicting pain. And at that point she wanted to inflict as much pain as possible.

"You need to stay focused, Nettie. We got a big job to do tomorrow and I need you focused, baby. You can't let things consume your mind. You need to be stronger than that," Wild said to her as he drove.

"I know," she said, blowing her nose with a tissue she got

out of the glove compartment. "But who would want to kill my brother? I mean, I know what he was, but everybody still loved and respected my brother, regardless of his addiction."

"Come on Nettie, you know what's up when you live the street life. You should know that." He looked over at her.

She didn't say a word. She continued to look straight ahead, wondering if her nephew and his friend made it back to the house safely.

"I'm gonna take you home, a'ight?"

"Yeah, but will you stay with me?" she asked him.

"And Maria won't have a problem with that?" He looked at her sideways, remembering why they never stayed at her place.

"At this point, the way that bitch is throwing shade, I don't give a fuck what she thinks. She is two seconds away from getting her ass slumped anyway." The anger seeped through Nettie's words.

Wild placed his hand on her thigh and rubbed it gently to calm her.

"Look at my shit!" She was referring to her fur coat. Her brother's blood showed visibly on the coat as a reminder of his death.

"It's gonna be a'ight, baby. I'm gonna take care of you," he assured her.

CHAPTER 44

Tyler and TJ had finally made it home. Tyler was afraid to go into the house, not wanting to have to explain to his mother where he had been. He didn't want to have to look in her face and tell her that her brother was dead. His heart was heavy with grief. He practically cried the whole way home. TJ kept trying to give him encouraging words, from his own experience of death in the family.

"I can't go home." Tyler sniffed.

"You can come over my house," TJ said sadly, feeling for his friend.

They both walked up the front steps and into the house.

Janet continued to drive around aimlessly. Things were getting out of control and she hated to lose control. Suddenly Janet's fears turned to rage the more she thought about the things that took place in the last couple of months. Her past was her past, but it seemed to always hover over her head as a constant reminder. She believed she'd served her time and paid her dues. Why were negative things like this always surrounding her? She felt the rage blinding her and cluttering her mind with all kinds of hateful things.

Dice and Click sat at the kitchen table in their apartment. They had a mass of weapons scattered on the table. Rows of ammunition were in boxes on the table as well. They were checking the functions of each weapon so they would be prepared and ready for the robbery the next night. They were both silent as a lit blunt clung to the corners of each of their mouths.

Shawnee and the other women had met Maria at the diner. Shawnee sat and explained to Maria how she felt about the way Nettie had thrown shade on them. But unbeknownst to Shawnee, Maria already knew the deal. Her cousins had already put her down about Shawnee and her way of thinking. They felt that Shawnee would be trouble for the crew. They knew that Nettie was an unpredictable person, but who didn't know that? They felt Nettie gave them the opportunity to make some real money and they were satisfied with that.

"So, do you see what I'm saying?" Shawnee asked Maria.

"Yeah, I see what you're saying, Shawnee. But you know Netta and she will have your head if you step to her with this BS."

"She can't kill all of us." Shawnee looked around the table at each of them.

"Don't look at me, Shawnee. I told you, I don't want

nothing to do with it," Yuming said.

"Then what the hell are you doing here?"

"I'm here because I want to make sure my name stays out of this petty crap," Yuming said seriously. Actually, she was making sure that none of them were trying to stab Nettie in the back. She admired Nettie and she understood her. Plus, Nettie didn't take anything off of anyone.

Shawnee rolled her eyes at Yuming and kept talking to the other women.

"So what do you want me to do?" Maria asked her. "Why didn't you just go to Netta with this instead of coming to me?"

"Because I tried, but she kept blowing me off, saying she was too busy. She probably was too busy with Wild bucking her up the ass."

"I've had enough of this." Yuming stood. "This is the very thing Nettie asked us not to do. We are supposed to be a team. You Americans are amazing. If we were in China, you would all be dead for even thinking of betraying your leader."

"That's the problem, bitch. We not in China; we in America and in America, if your leader is trying to play you, then you eliminate they ass," Shawnee said and meant every word.

"So now you want to kill your leader?" Yuming asked.

The others at the table were looking on, wide-eyed. They were actually shocked that Shawnee was bold enough to talk about killing Nettie in front of them.

"You will be sorry," Yuming said, and walked out of the restaurant.

"I don't think I want to have anything to do with this

either," Marisa said.

"Nettie don't put fear in my heart and neither does Yuming. I know she's going to tell Nettie but I don't care. I'm ready for whatever Nettie bringing," Shawnee said confidently.

Maria and the sisters walked out and left Shawnee in the restaurant to vent by herself.

Nettie sat on the sofa in the living room. Wild was sitting next to her, holding her. Neither of them said a word. They just sat there soaking in their own thoughts.

"I think I need to call that meeting I was supposed to have set up a long time ago," she said to Wild. "I think I'll have everyone meet me at the spot I had set up to hold the drugs. I think that's neutral ground for everybody. What do you think?"

"Yeah, maybe you should. It's seems like shit is fallin' apart and I need to get it back under control."

She looked at him and gave a weak smile.

"You go ahead and make the calls, babe, and when you're done come on in the bathroom so that I can bathe you." He winked at her.

She continued to smile at him. He got up from the sofa and went into the bathroom to run her bath water. Nettie made the necessary calls to every crewmember. It was finally set and everyone was to meet at the warehouse location in Newark.

-◁▷-◁▷-◁▷-

Janet saw someone walking up the street toward her as she drove. She pulled over to get the young man's attention. Once he got closer, she recognized him. She rolled down her window and blew the horn, waving him over to the car. He jogged over to the car and got in.

"What's up?" he asked.

"I can't find Tyler and I was wondering if you would be able to help me look for him?" she asked seriously.

"For sure, I can do that for ya," he said when his cell phone began to ring. He answered the phone and Janet pulled off from the curb, looking straight ahead.

CHAPTER 45

It was twelve midnight. The warehouse was abandoned and located in a dark area of an industrial section where rats, mice and other critters lurked in the darkness. Four luxury cars—a big-bodied Benz, which belonged to Meat; a BMW 760Li, which belonged to Click; a convertible BMW 650i, which belonged to Nettie; and a Bentley Arnage, which now belonged to Dice—were parked in a neat row in front of the warehouse's garage doors. A small amount of light could be seen through the ceiling-high windows of the warehouse.

Everyone had gathered in the warehouse except Nate who couldn't get away and needed to stay with Dak. Nettie thought it was a good idea for Nate to stay with Dak in order to ensure that Nate played Leroy's game. They were still scheduled to finish their plan accordingly.

The warehouse was filthy with dirt. It used to be a meat grinding factory and it obviously hadn't been used in several years. Rumor had it that back in the day organized crime leaders owned the factory. Supposedly they would use the factory to get rid of bodies.

The factory ground and packaged meats like beef, pork

and chicken. They even processed sausage and hot dogs. The rumor was that after grinding the dead or living bodies, the mobsters would mix the ground flesh with the ground animal meat and let the machines package all of it together. They did this so that there weren't any traces of the missing bodies. Then the packaged meat was distributed to the stores for sale.

Nettie stood in front of the meat grinder, facing her crew. Maria, Meat, Jasmine, Shawnee, Yuming and Marisa were all present. Dice and Click were there as well but they were out of sight. Little Cash hadn't arrived yet but he was on his way.

"I called everyone here today because the shit is about to blow. It may seem to you that I am not paying attention but I have ears and eyes out on them streets." Maria looked at Meat and he gave her a look to let her know that everything would be all right.

Maria had told Meat about the incident with Nettie in the dressing room. He was furious and never thought he would see the day when he wanted to snap Nettie in two. He knew that if he killed her, he would forever be on the run or would have to do the time in prison for his actions. Meat couldn't imagine doing time, so he told Maria to hold on until after the last job. They were going to take their money, leave town and start a new life somewhere far away from Nettie.

"I also know that some of you are feelin' some kind of way about the way I run this team." She paced back and forth.

Shawnee looked over at Yuming and the other women, knowing that somebody snitched. But Shawnee was no fool. She was prepared for what Nettie was bringing. Shawnee was packing heat and her two guns were cocked and ready. She smirked at Nettie real cocky-like. But Nettie kept pacing back and forth as she talked.

Nettie was not dressed in her usual expensive attire on this night. She had her hair pulled back neatly in a ponytail and was sporting a regular pair of body-hugging black jeans. She had on a tight-fitting, low-cut, white shirt with a thick, black belt pulled around her waist and over the shirt. She wore a black leather jacket and a pair of black, low-heeled riding boots.

"I told y'all in the beginning, before anything went down, that I wasn't for the bullshit. I said to you that if you had an issue with anyone, and that included me, that you needed to address the issue and squash it. I made myself perfectly clear on the rules of oath as well. But I see that muthafuckas like to do shit their own way. I guess y'all thought it was a game and tried to clown me, but the shit stops here. After we pull off the job tomorrow and I become the queen of the streets, I'm gonna make sure that whoever is on my team knows that this is not a game.

Shawnee rolled her eyes at Nettie. Maria narrowed her eyes. She couldn't believe that Nettie was standing there taking all the credit like none of them had helped. How could she possibly say she was going to be queen? Without them she would not have gotten as far as she did. *And she would have never gotten even that far without me,* Maria thought.

"So, to let y'all know this is not a game, before we go any further, this is just in case any of you forgot. I want to show y'all who the fuck I am." She stood there, mean-mugging them with that signature and sinister – Nettie-look.

"Dice! Click!" Nettie yelled. "Bring that muthafucka out here!" She turned back to look at the team's faces. She wanted to see their reactions.

Everyone began to stretch theirs necks trying to see who Nettie was talking about. Out from the back of the warehouse Dice and Click dragged a body. Jasmine put her hands over her mouth. She didn't know if the body was dead or alive. They held the man up from under his armpits with the front of his body facing the ground so no one knew who it was. Once they were in front of everyone, they dropped him to the hard cement floor. The man grunted loudly from hitting the hard floor.

Blood was everywhere. Dice grabbed him by the arm and turned him over onto his back. The women gasped when they saw the gruesome sight of Wild lying there in front of them. Meat held his head high in the air and looked straight ahead to avoid looking at him.

"This is who the fuck I am." Nettie pointed at Wild. "This nigga wouldn't listen to me when I told him that my brother wasn't no snitch. So he thought he would take matters into his own hands. Well, this is what happens to muthafuckas who think that they can clown Nettie."

Nettie knew it was Wild who killed her brother all along. When she saw him walking up the street, she recognized Wild's signature walk. She played the roll when he came back to the house with her. She was desperately hoping he would confess. Nettie loved him and would have forgiven him if he told her he killed James. She even thought that Wild coming into her life may have help to end her nightmare problem. Wild bought peace to her and she felt safe with him. But he betrayed her in the worst way and had to suffer.

When Wild went to run the bath water, Nettie called Dice and Click. She told them what happened and that she would leave the door unlocked for them to get in.

Nettie kicked Wild in the nuts. He yelled out in pain as he balled up into the fetal position.

"Muthafucka, you thought you was slick, didn't you? I'm that bitch!" She bent down to look in his face as she spoke.

His left eye was swollen shut and his nose looked like it was on the side of his face. Blood covered his face from the gash across his forehead. His lips were swollen and looked like balloons. Both his legs were broken and distorted. The blood ran from his forehead into his right eye and he squinted as he tried to look up at Nettie.

"Damn, Click, y'all busted dudes head open down to the white meat!" Nettie began to laugh in Wild's face.

Wild had been gathering saliva in his mouth so he spit in Nettie's face. It dripped down onto her white shirt, staining it with a pink and red splatter.

She stood quickly and began to wipe her face with the back of her hand. Shawnee snickered under her breath while everyone else was still looking on in shock.

"You fucked up my shit, Wild, and I'm feelin' some kind of way because of it. I'm not gonna play no more games wit' yo' ass. Get this nigga up and hang his ass on the pulley over there!" she instructed.

The pulley hung over the old meat grinder.

Dice and Click grabbed Wild and tried to lift him high enough to attach the hook to his belt but couldn't.

"What's up with you, Meat? They need your help. You just standing there like you ain't a part of this team. This nigga killed my brother!" Nettie screamed at him.

Meat moved, but he moved slowly. He grabbed Wild and lifted him like he was a feather. As he held Wild up in the air, Dice clamped the big hook to his belt. Meat stepped back and watched as Click hit the switch on the old machine.

Marisa screamed. She was startled and didn't expect the machine to work. But Nettie had the machine checked out when she made the deal for the warehouse after the first robbery. She had someone make sure the machine operated as she had contemplated having to use it. The monster machine began to come alive.

As Wild's body was being hoisted up into the air, Nettie looked into each of her crewmembers faces, satisfied with the reaction she was seeing.

Click was getting a kick out of this. He played with the chain, jerking Wild's body up and down, teasing him over the grinder. Wild hung there with his chin resting on his chest. His mouth hung open as string of saliva hung from his swollen bottom lip.

"Netta, please, we get the picture. Let him down. You can't be serious about this." Maria said.

"Yeah, Nettie, what kind of sick shit you into?" Shawnee asked, not so confident as she was just minutes earlier. Nettie let out a sinister laugh.

"Oh, y'all bitches got fear in ya hearts now, don't you? Oh, yeah, Shawnee, this is for you." Nettie pulled her gun from the inside pocket of her leather coat and shot Shawnee in the middle of her forehead. It was a perfect shot as Nettie had been going to the shooting range on the regular.

Jasmine began to scream and Marisa began to cry. Yuming had a smirk on her face as she watched Shawnee's body drop to the floor. Blood splatter flew on Maria because she stood the closet to Shawnee. She wiped her face and glared at Nettie.

Dice laughed. "Good for the bitch. I ain't like her ass anyway," he said.

Wild still hung on the pulley, half conscious as he moaned and groaned from his injuries.

"Nettie, why are you doing this?" Maria asked.

"Because, baby girl, I want the world to know that Nettie is a woman of her word." She sounded like an evil scientist.

"Nettie, what are you going to do, kill us all?" Meat asked her.

Nettie laughed. She then reached inside her jacket and pulled out another gun. She stood there with her legs apart, holding both guns down at her sides like she was ready for a western showdown.

"Meat, my old friend, you're still my boy, right?"

Meat never responded. He just stared at her with hatred filling his heart by each minute.

Nettie realized that Meat wasn't going to answer the question so she continued to talk.

"What if I did kill all y'all Meat, then what?" She toyed with him. She was disappointed in him. He was supposed to be loyal to her, not Maria.

"Meat, you kicked dirt on me by fuckin' my woman," she said.

"That's not true, Nettie," he lied in an attempt to calm her.

"Oh yes it is, Meat," she said as she raised her gun and shot Meat in the arm.

Nettie was out of control. She was on a power trip like no other. Maria began screaming at the top of her lungs. Meat stood there holding his arm, grimacing in pain. He glared at Nettie, ready to kill her.

"You bitch!" Maria had had enough. She ran and jumped on Nettie's back, putting her into the sleeper hold, a wrestling move that she learned watching *Smackdown* on TV. Nettie dropped the guns and tried to get Maria off of her. She spun around, trying to shake her off. She was getting light-headed and deprived of oxygen.

Out of nowhere, Yuming did a flying kick to Maria's back to get her off Nettie. Maria winced in pain and fell to the floor bringing Nettie down with her.

Yuming stood over her in a karate stance, ready to fight. A two-by-four came down across Yuming's back. She fell forward and came out of her fall by doing a forward roll. Yuming jumped to her feet and spun around to meet face to face with Jasmine who was still holding the wood she had picked up from the floor.

A grin came across Yuming's face. She was all too ready to fight, although she knew Jasmine was no competition.

"You Japanese bitch! You fuck with my family, you fuck with me," Jasmine said.

"I'm Chinese, you spic. Now show me what you got." Yuming smiled.

In the meantime, Nettie was still trying to get her bearings.

Jasmine charged at Yuming and she sidestepped, hitting

Jasmine in the back of the head with a karate chop and sent her flying, face first, to the cement floor.

This made Marisa come to her sister's rescue and charge Yuming. Yuming did a flying roundhouse and kicked Marisa in her face. Blood flew from Marisa's mouth as she hit the floor.

Dice and Click laughed. They got a kick out of the show they were watching.

Yuming stood there in her karate stance waiting for someone else to come at her so that she could bring more pain. Her adrenaline was working overtime. It had been awhile since she put her Black belt to use.

Nettie finally got herself together and went to stand by Yuming.

"You always been my girl, Yuming. I said it before and I'll say it again: If I had four more like you, we would be unstoppable. This is what I call loyal!" Nettie announced.

Just then the doors to the warehouse opened. Nettie, Dice and Click pointed their guns toward the door. Little Cash walked in with Janet trailing behind him.

Everyone in the room except Meat and Maria stood there in total disbelief.

"Cash, what are you doing with my sister?" Nettie asked.

"No, the question is what are you doing, Nettie?" Janet asked as she went and stood in front of Nettie.

Everyone's mouth hung open. They couldn't believe their eyes. The twins looked at each other as if mirror images. Nettie and Janet were identical twins. With Nettie wearing her hair pulled back into a neat ponytail, she was the spitting image of Janet since she wore her hair that way all the time.

"Oh, shit, Cash was right," Dice whispered to Click, who was looking stuck on stupid.

Meat and Maria were the only two who knew that Nettie had an identical twin sister.

"I always gotta come to your rescue and save your ass, don't I?" Janet asked, eyeballing Nettie.

"What are you talking about?" Nettie asked her. "Did you find Tyler?"

"No, I didn't find Tyler. Don't try to change the subject. Haven't I done enough for you, Nettie?"

Everyone looked on and wondered what was going on.

"Look at you. You got a dead body lying here and I'm sure homeboy hanging up there is on his last leg. Why are you so sloppy? I thought I taught you better than that," Janet spat, reprimanding her twin.

"Janet, not now. I got business to take care of." She turned her back on her sister, grabbed a handful of Maria's hair and snatched her up.

"I told you to get rid of that bitch a long time ago. She knows too much," Janet said.

"Let her go, Nettie," Meat demanded, still holding his arm. Janet laughed.

"You feeling her, Meat?" Janet asked.

Janet snatched Maria from Nettie's grip, spit a blade in her hand and cut Maria from ear to ear.

"Nooooo!" Meat screamed as he charged toward Nettie and Janet.

Jasmine and Marisa began to scream as well. Dice and Click opened fire on Meat, trying to stop him from getting to Nettie. Nettie also raised her guns and began to shoot but

Meat was like a machine. His body jerked as each bullet hit him, but he kept taking steps forward until he finally fell to his knees in front of them. He fell face forward and landed next to Maria.

Jasmine and Marisa were crying hysterically by then. Nettie looked over at her sister and then back at Maria.

"I know you not gonna stand there and act like you still sweet on that bitch?" Janet asked Nettie.

Nettie just stared at her sister, not saying a word. She was hurt. Regardless of how she treated Maria at times, she genuinely did care about her.

"Yo, this shit is nuts!" Click said, amped. "Nett, I ain't know you had a twin. This shit is like something straight outta a movie!"

"Word up," Dice agreed.

CHAPTER 46

Jasmine and Marisa sat holding each other as they whimpered and mourned for their dead cousin. Yuming still stood confident with her hands on her hips. Little Cash wore a look of contempt on his face. He was wondering what the hell he had walked into. When he got the phone call from Nettie to meet at the warehouse, he was in the car with Janet. He decided to tell her what was going on. He trusted her and thought that she would be able to help him. Plus, she insisted on coming. Now that he saw how Janet and Nettie worked together, he wondered if talking to Janet that day at her house and bringing her to the warehouse was a good idea.

Little Cash had a feeling that Nettie killed Beverly and Desiree that day at the cemetery. Rumors spread that it was Nettie because of the way they were killed. Little Cash heard the same rumors but dismissed them until that day he went with Nettie to visit her mother and saw the baby. He knew in his mind that there was no way that was Nettie's baby. He had a gut feeling that it was Ishmael and Desiree's baby when he saw the strong resemblance to Ishmael. He had seen Desiree a few times after Ishmael was murdered and knew she was carrying his baby. But he never saw her again before she was killed.

Little Cash needed to be sure that Nettie was the killer. He had no idea what he would have done if he found out that Nettie actually killed Beverly and Desiree. He knew that they needed to get that baby from her. It was no secret to most that Nettie hated Ishmael so why would she want his seed living with her family? What was she hiding? Did she kill Ishmael? These questions had run through his mind a thousand times, driving him crazy. He decided to talk to Janet, thinking she was a reasonable person. But now, as he looked around the warehouse, he realized that talking to Janet might have been a bad idea.

"Damn, Nette, ya sister spits blades too, huh?" Click asked.

Janet looked at Nettie and then back at Click.

"Sweetheart, how do you think Nettie learned how to spit a blade?" Janet smiled an evil grin.

It was true. Janet was the master when it came to using blades, knives or any weaponry. Unbeknownst to most, she was also a martial artist. Janet and Nettie were born fifteen minutes apart and Janet was the oldest. There was a saying that with twins you had a good one and a bad one. Well in the case of the Wright sisters, Nettie was always the sweet and caring girl, whereas Janet was the dark and devious one. Growing up, Nettie loved Janet with all her heart. She admired how she was bold and outspoken. Janet always stood up for Nettie, protecting her from the cruel kids that would take advantage of her.

They hadn't always lived in Essex County. They were born in Macon, Georgia and their mother moved them to New Jersey when they were thirteen. Since then they've moved several times during their teens. The fast life of the city was exciting to Janet and right up her alley. She adjusted to New Jersey quickly but Nettie shied away from it. Janet realized that Nettie was going to have to get a backbone and defend herself. So with the knowledge and skills Janet learned from being in gangs and fighting, she taught her sister how to defend herself. Janet was a master at using a blade and she taught Nettie how to carry the blade in her mouth as well. After countless times of Nettie cutting the inside of her mouth, she was trained and ready for the streets by the age of fifteen. By then Janet had dropped out of school and was lost in the streets, living on the edge. She barely came home and when she did it was to drop in and check on her sister.

When they were older, Janet did five years in jail for her sister. Nettie did the crime but Janet did the time for the sister she loved so much. Nettie had gotten into a confrontation with the wife of the man she'd been fucking. It wasn't that Nettie was spent on the man. She liked him because he was ballin' out and trickin' his money on her for sex. Nettie never anticipated that the wife would be deranged. She came after Nettie with all she had, and all she had were her two sisters. They jumped Nettie and beat her down. When Nettie got her own sister to get the women back, Janet was more than happy to oblige after seeing her sister's condition.

They waited for three weeks and got each woman one at a time. But when it came time to seek revenge on the wife, she gave Nettie a hard time. Janet was there to assist when the woman scratched Nettie across her right eye in a dirty attempt to win the fight. This left the wife and Janet to fight a fair one but the wife was no slouch when it came to brawling either. As they fought the wife began to overpower Janet. Nettie regained her sight, saw the fight starting to go against her sister, and she lost control. Nettie spit her blade and started slicing. When it was all over, the wife was damned near dead. They fled the scene only to have the police come to their home the next day to make an arrest from a witness statement. They came to arrest Nettie but when they saw Janet, they weren't sure who actually committed the crime. The police only had a physical description, so that meant either one could be guilty. Janet stepped up and took the punishment for her sister.

When Janet went away to jail all she asked Nettie to do was take care of their mother and her two small children. Nettie made the promise but never kept it. Nettie was wild, carefree and simply didn't follow through. In fact, she never visited her sister when she was locked up. Janet felt like Nettie had turned her back on her when she needed her the most.

When Janet came home she was rehabilitated. She had learned that the life she led was not the right way. She studied the Bible while being incarcerated and had turned over a new leaf. Janet began to look at life in a new light and wanted her children to do the same. She vowed by hook or crook she would make sure her children were not exposed to the dark side of life. She wanted to give them a better opportunity and a chance at succeeding.

Unfortunately, she was only able to move them from one hood to another, but that didn't stop her from making sure they were raised with morals. She made sure that she schooled them and kept them from harm's way. But there was an 80 percent chance that a child growing up in the hood would eventually fall victim to the street life. Janet wanted to make sure her children fell well within that 20 percent that made it out of the hood successfully.

Little Cash noticed that everyone was preoccupied so he decided to take advantage of the moment to get out of there. He began to slowly back peddle, while keeping a watchful eye on everyone. Jasmine and Marisa stood holding each other tightly and crying for their lives. In their minds they knew that they would be the next ones to die.

"Janet, I can take care of myself. You always stepping on my toes. I got this," Nettie said.

"I can't tell, Nettie. Your shit is fall apart at the seams right now," Janet said, looking her up and down. "And what are you going to do with homeboy up there?" she asked as if she was Nettie's mother.

Nettie rolled her eyes. Janet was doing it again. She was trying to control Nette Janet always did this to Nettie. This was one of the reasons why Nettie stayed away from her family. It was one of the reasons why Nettie couldn't stand her sister, but she feared her. Janet never let Nettie live down how she took the charge for *her*.

Nettie stood. "Janet, I got this and I don't need your help."

"Oh, you got this, huh?" Janet eyed her.

"Yeah."

"So just tell me what you're doing, Nettie."

"This is my crew and I run shit, so fuck what you heard!" Nettie was confident.

"Oh, this ya crew?" Janet laughed. "So what, you gonna kill everybody in the crew?"

"No, Janet! I'm teaching the ones that aren't loyal a lesson."

"Well, my dear better half of a sister, then you should have started with him." She turned behind her and pointed to Little Cash who was halfway to the door.

Little Cash stopped in his tracks when everyone turned to look at him.

"What are you talking about, Janet?" Nettie asked.

"Ya boy over there came to me ready to rat you out, my sister. Yeah, he was spilling his guts to me like I was some kind of psychiatrist or something." Janet chuckled.

Nettie looked at Little Cash with unbelieving eyes. She had always liked Little Cash and she always took up for him. She knew if no one else was loyal, Little Cash was a good dude.

"I don't believe you," Nettie said.

"Well you better, because ya boy over there knows about the baby and he knows that you killed Desiree." Janet spilled the beans in front of everyone.

Nettie was furious. Her blood was beginning to heat up. How could her sister reveal such a deep secret in front of everyone? She had no idea if everyone knew. She had been living in her sister's shadow for far too long. Nettie broke away to make a name for herself, to have individuality. But, in the back of her mind she always knew she would be indebted to Janet for the things she had done for her.

Dice and Click looked at each other dumbfounded. They couldn't believe their ears. Little Cash was right again. This new information brought different feelings about Nettie.

"She lying!" was all Little Cash could come up with to say. At that point anything he said was null and void because told Janet everything.

"Cash, I thought you were my boy." Nettie said, disappointed in him, but ready to kill him for betraying her.

CHAPTER 47

Detective Daniels was just about ready to call it a night, thinking the suspect wasn't going to show, when he got a call over the radio. A security patrolman had been patrolling the industrial area and spotted several luxury cars sitting in front of the warehouse. Most of the buildings in that area were abandoned, so he questioned the activity in the old building. He looked inside, witnessed the horrifying murders and called it in.

Detective Daniels floored the gas pedal and the unmarked police vehicle floated through the streets.

"Why did you kill Beverly and Desiree? You wrong for that, Nette, and you know it. What did they ever do to you?" Little Cash was pissed now that he knew the truth. "Did you kill Ish too?"

Nettie was on fire. How dare this little punk question her when she was the one who put him on? She was the only one who took up for him when everyone else was ready to dig his grave.

"I didn't kill Ish! But you kicked my back in, Cash, and I can't let that go. No way, no how, homeboy," Nettie said demonically as she began to walk slowly toward Little Cash.

"So what you gonna do? Kill me too, Nette? I got little brothers and a sister to take care of. My mother is dying, Nette. This shit is gonna hafta stop somewhere." Cash was trying anything to save his life.

Dice and Click looked at each other and neither of them knew what to do. Nate wasn't there and he usually made the decisions.

"Yo, for real, Nette is off the chain," Click whispered to Dice.

"So what do you think we should do?" Dice asked Click.

"Man, fuck Cash, for real. Nettie is the truth. Just chill, she got this."

Dice shook his head up and down, but he wasn't so sure that was the right thing to do. But what choice did he have? So the two of them stood and watched as Nettie approached Little Cash.

Little Cash had begun to back away slowly as Nettie approached him. She looked into his eyes and saw the deep hurt that Little Cash was feeling. But she couldn't let him get away with trying to destroy her. Her ego would not allow it and now that Janet was involved, Nettie knew she had to kill Little Cash.

She stood in front of him with her arm extended, holding the Glock with a steady hand. Little Cash stood still as if he was going out like a soldier but tears were rolling down his face.

"Do it already!" Janet yelled.

"Why don't you chill out and let Nettie do what she do?"

Yuming asked Janet.

She had been standing there the whole time taking it all in. Not once had she said a word about the situation. But enough was enough. Yuming felt that it was an insult to Nettie, the way Janet walked in, and dominated the situation. Yuming was raised to give respect, and respecting family was number one. But from what she was seeing and hearing, Janet was controlling Nettie because she took a charge for her years ago. Yuming believed that was what family was supposed to do for each other and she was not going to stand there and let Janet walk all over her friend.

"You talking to me?" Janet asked Yuming.

"You're the only one standing here running ya mouth," Yuming said. "Why are you disrespecting your sister in front of her team?"

Janet laughed. "Team?" She looked around at the scene. "This team is a joke." She continued to laugh.

If Yuming was a dragon she would have been breathing fire. On pure reflex, Yuming punched Janet in the side of the face. Janet took a couple steps to the side from the impact of the blow. She held her hand to the side of her face and smiled at Yuming who got into her karate stance, ready to spar. Nettie turned around to see what was going on.

Little Cash took that opportunity to run for the door. When Nettie turned back around and realized Cash had taken off, she aim her gun and shot Little Cash in the back. At that moment Janet struck out at Yuming since she was looking at Nettie. Janet threw a kick to Yuming's head. Yuming blocked the kick and came back with a kick of her own. Janet side-stepped the kick and the two women began to circle each other. They studied each other, anticipating the next move.

Little Cash lay on his stomach, moaning from the pain of the bullet wound.

"Janet, what are you doing?" Nettie shouted as she walked toward the two women.

"This bitch got the right one fucking with me. Bring it!" Janet said to Yuming.

Yuming simply smirked at Janet as she lunged forward. They threw punches at each other and blocked punches equally before separating.

"You got skills," Yuming said. She was impressed. Janet just laughed at Yuming.

"Janet, leave her alone! I am so sick of your shit!" But they didn't listen to Nettie. They just kept fighting.

"Freeze! Don't nobody move!" Detective Daniels said, standing inside the warehouse with two uniformed policemen. One of the officers went to check on Little Cash and his actions caught everyone's attention. Detective Daniels looked around at the dead bodies and then turned his attention toward Wild still hanging. His facial expressions showed disgust.

"Rick, what are you doing here?" Janet asked, totally changing into a different person.

"Janet, words cannot express how disappointed I am in you right now," he said sincerely.

"What are you talking about? I came here to try to save my sister from these thugs," she lied.

"Well, I've been waiting to see you," he said.

"This one's gone, detective," the uniformed officer said,

referring to Little Cash.

"Janet, I have a warrant for your arrest."

"For what?" She looked shocked.

Nettie looked back at the detective who had been staring back and forth between her and Janet, not believing his eyes. Detective Daniels had no knowledge of Janet and Nettie being twins either. He knew about Nettie from the things Janet had told him, but she never mentioned that they were twins. Now he remembered seeing Nettie and mistaking her for Janet. He saw her driving the BMW when he answered the call about James being shot.

"For the murder of Beverly Downing," Detective Daniels answered.

The results had come back on the finger prints after time consuming hours and it was a match to her. Detective Daniels would have never guessed the woman he was in love with was not rehabilitated, but still very much a criminal. He always had reservations when he first met her in jail. But her personality convinced him that he was wrong. Janet was a model prisoner and Detective Daniels was able to visit her often. The two would converse on many occasions since she was housed in a low-risk section of the prison. Detective Daniels adored her and believed in a person changing. He knew how she was raised and understood her struggle with finding herself while growing up. Once she was released they became inseparable until he was promoted to detective.

Dice and Click looked at each other.

"We gotta get up outta dodge," Click whispered to Dice, who gave him a head nod.

Janet's face turned to rage. Once again she had been helping Nettie and again she would take the fall.

When Nettie came to Janet about Zola being murdered, Janet could see the devastation on her sister's face. She knew exactly how her sister felt about Zola and Janet knew the pain she was feeling. Nettie told Janet that she was ready to kill everybody that had anything to do with Ishmael. Janet was the level-headed of the two and she knew Nettie had no idea how to deal with the situation. Janet and Nettie had what most would call a love-hate type of relationship. It was as easy for them to love and hate each other. But their love was unconditional, even during the times they hated one another.

Janet had decided to help her sister get revenge once again. They plotted and waited for a year before striking. That day when they followed Desiree and Beverly into the cemetery, they were dressed identical to each other just in case there were any witnesses. When Nettie headed up the hill after Desiree, Janet was supposed to a watch out for Beverly. But as Janet sat there, waiting her cruel mind began to turn. Janet decided to take care of Beverly while Nettie took care of Desiree.

When Nettie came back to the car she saw Beverly hanging from the open passenger door as blood poured from her neck onto the ground. She looked around for her sister who was nowhere to be found. Nettie heard the whining and whimpering of the baby from inside the car. She removed the baby from Desiree's car and took the baby with her.

Nettie felt that if Janet hadn't killed Beverly, the baby would have been okay. But since Janet took matters into her own hands, Nettie took the baby to her mother's house. Although Nettie seemed to be a heartless person, she couldn't leave the baby in the car alone Janet didn't like the idea but had no other choice at the time. The sisters made an agreement that they both would raise the child but Nettie once again reneged. This brought their hatred for each other to the surface once again.

CHAPTER 48

Detective Daniels and Janet eyed each other although he could barely stand to look at her. He loved her dearly and he knew she loved him but the beast that lurked in Janet had never left her soul. They would never be able to build a relationship based on her cruel actions. He was a cop and took his job seriously so he had to do it with no feelings involved.

"Janet, I'm sorry but I'm gonna have to take you in," he said, walking toward her. "I need the rest of you to drop your weapons and place your hands on your heads."

Janet stood there as her face became red with anger. She refused to go back to jail. She grabbed a gun from Nettie's hands and began to fire at Detective Daniels and the other officers. Everyone dove for cover. Click managed to slip to the back of the warehouse and make it out the backdoor, disappearing into the fields behind it. Dice started firing his weapon at the officers. Jasmine and Marisa dropped to the floor covering their heads as they screamed loudly. Neither of them had a gun so they were sitting ducks in the middle of a gun battle and they figured their lives were over. Yuming managed to slip behind one of the machines for cover.

Nettie began to shoot at the three police officers. Detective Daniels and the two uniformed officers ducked and hit the floor. Nettie turned and ran behind one of the machines.

Stray bullets hit Wild, killing him as he continued to hang from the pulley. A small pool of blood had dropped from his wounds and settled on the cement floor. Dice slipped and fell in the pool of blood while trying to run for cover. He slammed the back of his head on the cement floor and cracked his skull, killing him instantly.

The shooting battle continued and Nettie knew that it was a losing battle. As two more uniformed officers arrived on the scene, she began to plot her getaway. She signaled for Yuming to come to her. Yuming slithered her way over to Nettie.

"Yuming, I need to get outta here. I can't go out like this. Where does your loyalty lie?" Nettie asked her.

Yuming knew what her friend was asking her to do. She knew Nettie wanted her to get her out of the warehouse, even if it meant she had to give her life. Yuming simply nodded and hugged Nettie. She knew this would probably be the last time they would see each other.

Janet ran out of ammunition, so she crawled over to where Dice lay and pried the gun from his dead hands. She sat there with her back against the machine that was still running. The gunfire had ceased and Detective Daniels used hand motions to direct his men to make their way around the warehouse. He signed to them to find and arrest everyone.

In the meantime, Nettie and Yuming were crouched

down and trying to work their way through the rubble and machinery, heading for the backdoor. Nettie was in front of Yuming because Yuming's sharp senses would let her know if trouble was approaching from behind them. More policemen arrived and surrounded the warehouse.

Janet could see the additional police arriving through the small space in between the machines. She wondered where her sister was and if she was still alive. She could see Jasmine and Marisa lying in the middle of the floor covering their heads for protection.

Just then Detective Daniels's radio began to go off. It was the dispatcher letting him know that there was no contact information for the family of James Wright, also known as Black Santa. Detective Daniels turned off his radio. He knew all along that James was Janet's brother, but Janet had no idea that James was an informant. It was the first she heard of her brother's death.

Suddenly Janet felt alone. She didn't have her sister by her side, and she thought Nettie was betraying her once again. She had stood by Nettie's side all her life and couldn't understand her sister's deceit. Who was there to stand by her side now? She may have been disappointed in the way her brother led his life, but that didn't mean she didn't love him. She shed a few tears and then wiped them away. Janet stood and made herself visible. She held the gun to her head as she stared Detective Daniels in the eyes.

"Hold your fire!" he instructed the officers. He walked out into the open. "Janet, don't do this," he pleaded.

Janet didn't say a word. She stood in front of the detective; sweat covered and crazed expression on her face. There was no life in her eyes.

"Janet, baby, please, I can help you. Don't you do it!" He noticed a uniformed officer attempting to move closer. "Move back! I said hold your fire!" He instructed the men again.

"Help me?" Janet whispered. "How can you help me, Rick? I'm an ex-con and a murderer. There is no help for me."

Detective Daniels put his gun down at his side and held his hand out to Janet.

"Janet, take the gun away from your head, baby. Let me have it." he told her.

Janet saw another police officer try to move around the detective.

"I'll do it. Stay away from me!" she warned.

"Stay right there and don't move!" Detective Daniels told the officer.

Nettie and Yuming continued to move slowly and quietly. When they finally made it to the rear door, Nettie turned just in time to see Janet remove the gun from her head and shoot Detective Daniels in the chest. Yuming pushed Nettie out the backdoor as the other officers began to open fire on Janet, sending her bullet-riddled body flying into the machinery.

Detective Daniels lay on the cold floor holding his chest. Two of the officers ran over to assist him. One officer ripped his coat and shirt open, and saw his body armor, intact. They both breathed a sigh of relief.

Outside in the back of the warehouse Yuming and Nettie lay flat on their stomachs in the tall weeds. Nettie still held on to one of her guns. She was ready to take aim at one of the three officers looking around the grounds.

Yuming crawled forward, not making a sound. It was almost as if she knew where to step. She was within a few feet from one of the officers, as he searched the tall weeds and rubble with a flashlight. Yuming removed a star from her belt and whizzed it at the officer, hitting him in the neck. He opened his mouth but no sound came out as he fell to the ground. The other two police officers never heard a sound as they continued to search the area.

Yuming then worked her way back to Nettie.

"Nettie, you are going to have to make a run for it while I distract them," Yuming said.

"There are two of them, Yuming. Why don't you let me take them out while I got a clear shot."

"No, Nettie, the others will hear the gunfire and come to assist them. No, you give me the gun and I will distract them. Stay low to the ground and get outta here." Yuming said seriously as she looked at Nettie.

Nettie handed Yuming the gun and prepared run at Yuming's signal.

"Can you shoot a gun?" Nettie thought to ask.

"We will find out, won't we?" Yuming winked at Nettie.

They both smiled at each other and Yuming moved away from her. She stood up once she was a far enough distance away from Nettie.

"Hey, looking for me?" Yuming stood there with her hands behind her back, concealing the gun and a mini knife she held.

Both officers shined their flashlights at Yuming. Nettie took off running through the tall weeds. One of the officers heard her and aimed his light in her direction as Yuming opened fire on the officer, striking him in the shoulder and in the chest. Yuming then dove to the ground, concealing herself in the weeds. The other officer fired his gun and kept firing as he tried to find her with his flashlight. Just as Yuming said, other officers heard the gunfire and came running to assist.

Yuming managed to shoot another officer and threw her knife in the stomach of yet another officer before she was gunned down instantly killed.

CHAPTER 49

Nettie made it back to her apartment where she changed her clothes and threw a few items into a duffel bag. She had tried to call Nate several times while heading home but got no answer. She left him a message letting him know that she was going to get outta town. She told him to call her as soon as he got the message and grabbed another duffel bag filled with money. She threw a fitted cap on her head and headed out of the apartment knowing that someone would soon figure out where she resided.

She ran down the street to the garages where the residents of the apartment building parked. Nettie went into the garage and got into her old BMW that she was planning to give to Maria. She pulled out and was heading toward the turnpike with no destination in mind when her cell phone rang. She looked at the caller ID and saw that it was Nate.

"Nate, where you at?" she asked.

"Nettie, what the fuck is going on?" he asked.

"Nate, shit went all wrong. I gotta get outta town for a while."

"Where you at, Nettie?"

"I'm heading to the turnpike."

"What are you driving?"

"I'm driving my old beamer," she said.

"Naw, Nette, meet me at my house. I'll give you one of my whips to drive. It's too risky to let you drive your own joint," Nate advised.

"Okay, how long before you get there?"

"I'll be there in five minutes. Park your joint around the corner and come through the backdoor. I'll leave it open," he told her.

"Aight, Nate, I'll be there. Hey, Nate," she called into the phone.

"Yeah?"

"Thanks man," she said.

"No doubt. One."

Fifteen minutes later, Nettie was walking in the backdoor of Nate's apartment. He met her in the kitchen as she entered and gave her a warm hug.

"You aight?" he asked, looking her up and down.

"Yeah, I'm good."

"Aight, come on. We gotta go by Dice and Click's apartment, 'cause that's where the car at," he said, grabbing the keys to his car and walking toward the backdoor.

"Did you know that Dice is dead, Nate?" Nettie asked as she followed behind him, walking out the door.

"Yeah, I know all about it. Click called me. He's gonna lay low for a while too," Nate said.

They made it to Click's apartment where the car was located. Once they got there Click came outside and backed the car out of the driveway while Nettie got out of Nate's car.

"Get in, Nettie," Click said.

"What are you doing, Click?" she asked.

"Listen, I gotta go underground, too so we might as well do it together."

"I think that's a good idea," Nate said. "I'll keep in touch with y'all to let y'all know what's going on," he assured them.

Nettie gave her bags to Nate. While he placed them on the backseat she got in the passenger's side and was ready to go. Nate gave Nettie a kiss on the cheek and he gave Click a pound. He stepped away from the car and Click took off down the street.

They traveled in silence, each reliving the night's events. A strange feeling came over Nettie as if someone was watching her. She looked over at Click who seemed to be deep in thought. She couldn't shake the creepy feeling. Silently, a leather belt slipped over her head and tightened around her neck. Her head was pinned to the headrest and pressure was applied, holding her head steady. Nettie tried to reach behind her and grab her assailant but to no avail. She scratched and clawed, trying to get Click to help her. But he simply moved out of her reach. Her eyes grew in size as her lungs were deprived of air.

A shocked look came across Nettie's face and her mouth stretched wide open. But nothing came out of her mouth except gurgling sounds. Blood ran from her neck when the tip of an ice pick, broke through her skin. After a few more minutes of struggling, Nettie was dead.

Click looked in the backseat at the killer who had been lying underneath covers on the floor of the car. TJ looked over at Click, and then turned his attention to the window.

"I guess your mother's soul can rest in peace now," Click finally said to the young boy.

"Indeed," was all TJ said as he continued to stare out the window.

Although Janet had killed his mother, Beverly, Nate and Click felt that Nettie needed to go as well. After hearing the whole story, they believed that Nettie may have had something to do with Ishmael's death, too.

Dice told Nate about what he found out from Little Cash and Nate decided to investigate it. Although he told Dice to let it go and let Ishmael's soul rest, Nate still felt something wasn't right. He went over to Nettie's mother's house and found TJ coming home from school. He called him over to the car and talked with him for a few. He realized that Tyler was Nettie's nephew and used TJ to get some inside information. Nate took the young boy for a ride and found out that Little Cash had told the truth. But Nate wanted more proof, so he kept the information to himself and decided to wait it out.

Nate knew TJ's mother, Beverly, very well. But who didn't? Beverly was the 411 of the hood and couldn't keep her mouth shut. Then Click called Nate after escaping the warehouse and told him all that went down. Click didn't know the fate of the others but when Nettie called; Nate knew that she had escaped. He quickly put a plan together so the young TJ could get revenge for his mother's death.

CHAPTER 50

One year later •

Once the news hit the streets of what happened at the warehouse, Dak called Leroy and told him to stay where he was for a while. Dak took over and ran the business for Leroy until his return. Leroy had gone south to get dirt on Detective Daniels from the old mayor. But after the warehouse incident, Detective Daniels turned down the heat from Leroy.

Nate and Click had used the money that they had saved along with the profits that the crew had incurred, to start a legit business. They opened up an armed security company that employed over fifty people. Of course it was a front for what they really did. Leroy gave them their own territory that they supplied. Click was still his usual, hot-headed self, but Nate had managed to tame the savage beast and learned how to deal with people in a business matter. But on the streets he was still nuts. Although they didn't work directly for Leroy anymore, he was their supplier. Through telephone conversations and with Dak's assistance, Leroy gave Nate pointers along with personal contacts to help him flourish in his legitimate business.

Jasmine and Marisa were arrested that night at the warehouse but released later due to lack of evidence. They both told the same story: They were kidnapped and brought to the warehouse against their will.

Tyler never stopped dealing drugs, even after the death of his mother, aunt and uncle. He seemed to go off the deep end and threw himself even deeper into the game. He teamed up with another up-and-coming young crew of gettin'-money niggas. He was finally able to do what it was he wanted to do and had a new whip, fly clothes and Shorties surrounding him even though he wasn't of legal age. Tyler had finally gained the respect that he fought so hard to get. He was killed only seven months after his family was laid to rest.

Carolyn Wright ended up in a mental institution. After all her children and grandson died, she lost it. She wasn't stable or physically able to take care of baby Nyeem or Naeesha. Naeesha was put into foster care and adopted by a young couple who couldn't have children. She was now living in a two-parent, middle class home in the suburbs, filled with lots of love.

⋖⋑⋖⋑⋖⋑

As for TJ, he threw himself into school determined to get his diploma and further his education. He was going to pursue his law degree or die trying. He still had dreams about his mother's death but at least at the end of his dreams his mother had a smile on her face. He did save a good piece of change from his hustling days, as well as the money Nate hit him off with for doing Nettie. So, he would have enough money to get into a decent college. He often mourned his friend's death, especially when he sat on the porch after he finished his homework. But TJ was a smart kid and he knew that the type of lifestyle he chose to live could ultimately be the end of his life.

Detective Daniels still drove the streets of Newark, chasing drug dealers, murderers and thieves. Blist remained calm and watched his friend drive himself crazy, chasing his tail like a dog. But Detective Daniels loved his job and the thrill of the chase more than life itself.

Today, Leroy sat in his usual spot behind his desk as he talked with Dak about business. Dak was still his right-hand man but he no longer headed up security. Dak was now his business partner. A knock came at the door and Leroy's new head of security poked his head inside.

"Some cat named Nate is out here to see you," the burly man said.

"Yeah, yeah, that's my man. Let him in," Leroy instructed.

Nate walked in the door with a smile on his face, holding the hand of an eighteen-month-old child.

"What's good, Big Roy? You finally made it back into

town, huh?" Nate asked, extending his one free hand.

Leroy stared at Nate and the child who was holding his hand.

"I've been back in town for a couple months now, young blood. How's business? Where you been?" Leroy asked. Nate gave Dak a pound and took a seat.

"Business is aight. I been a little busy myself." Nate smiled as he placed the child on his lap.

"What you got there, son? That's you?" Leroy asked, staring at Nyeem.

"Naw, but this here is little Ish." Nate looked down at the boy.

"He looks just like him." Leroy was amazed.

"For sure. This gonna be my little man right here." Nate continued to look down at the toddler.

While Click and TJ took care of Nettie that night, Nate was on his way to Nettie's mother's house to get baby Nyeem. When Carolyn came to the door, Nate simply told her he was the father of the baby and she happily allowed him to take the baby and all of his belongings.

Leroy and Dak looked at each other. Leroy was overwhelmed as he looked at his grandson. To this day, no one knew that Leroy was Ishmael's father, except Dak.

"Where you get him from? I had no idea Ish had a son," Dak said, not revealing that he knew all along.

"Well pull up a chair, Dak, and I'll tell you all about it," Nate instructed.

Dak sat in the chair next to Nate while Leroy continued to marvel over the toddler.

"So you gonna raise him?" Dak asked.

"Yeah, I'm gonna keep him close and teach him all he

needs to know. Nyeem will be the next HNIC of Essex County. He will follow right in his father's footsteps but he will succeed. No offense to you, Big Roy," Nate said.

"None taken, young blood, none taken," Leroy said as he proudly looked at his grandson.

BOOK CLUB DISCUSSION QUESTIONS

1. Now that you've read the book and have a little understanding about Nettie, do you think her and her sister Janet's upbringing played a major role in the women they became? Were they raised in a dysfunctional family in your opinion? Why or why not?

2. Do you think Meat and Maria deserved to die? Why or why not?

3. It is said that money is the root of all evil. Do you think that played a major part in this novel that led to the characters making the decisions that they did? Explain.

4. Nettie and Wild seemed to have the same mindset. With the small amount of time that they've known each other it seemed they fell in love. Is love only found in honest people?

5. Detective Daniels loved his job and his girlfriend Janet. Janet loved him as well and with Detective Daniels knowing about her past. Do you think he should have handled the situation differently allowing her live? Why or why not?

6. What are your thoughts on Tyler and TJ?

7. It is said that 90% of male children born into poverty with one parent or raised by a guardian will turn to a life of crime. What are your thoughts on these statistics and what do you think if anything can be done to change this?

8. With a sick mother and younger siblings, what are your thoughts on Little Cash? Do you believe that he would have walked away from it all if given the opportunity?

9. Who was your favorite character in the novel? Explain why.

10. Who was your least favorite character in the book? Explain why.

11. In 2006 Newark, NJ's murder rate by the end of the year was 2839 in murders. In 2006 Newark rated higher in violent crimes such as murder, robbery, burglary, aggravated assaults vehicular thefts and forcible rapes mostly drug related. The media can't possibly show you the everyday lives in the hood on television or in the newspaper. Do you believe the crimes that happened in the novel are true to life? Why or why not?

Visit us online

for excerpts, videos, discounts,

photos, and author information.

MelodramaPublishing.com

Also visit us on MySpace and Facebook

Get HOOD

978-1934157572   978-1934157589   978-1934157596

Just $6.99 each!

MelodramaPublishing.com